ME AND KEV

ME AND KEV

A NOVEL BY

SIMON BLACK

BASKERVILLE
PUBLISHERS, INC.
DALLAS • NEW YORK • DUBLIN

BASKERVILLE Publishers, Inc.
7540 LBJ/Suite 125, Dallas, TX 75251-1008

Library of Congress Catalog Card Number: 93-70995
ISBN: 1-880909-08-1

Manufactured in the United States of America
First Printing

for Margaret Black and Henry Black

I
STORIES

MY DEATH

I didn't know what it meant, but around my eighth year of life I noticed that it was missing—an important part of my body. Perhaps I had never had one, perhaps it had fallen off. For a second I thought of rushing into my parents' room and telling them. Then I felt the empty space at the bottom of my stomach again—ran my fingers over it— and was ashamed.

I hid my disability from the world. I never took my shirt off on sunny days like the other children. I never went swimming in the swimming hole. In gym class I lurked in a dark corner of the locker room to change my clothes in case a bully or a clown spotted my peculiar lack. Nobody knew my terrible secret.

Otherwise I lived a normal life on the farm with my mother and father, spending most of my time playing different games by myself and running around like a chicken, and it didn't matter that I didn't have what everyone else had. It was a useless appendage, after all. Not having one didn't stop you from climbing trees or munching cookies or killing squirrels with stones. Not having one didn't make any difference at all, I thought.

But one day in high summer in my eleventh year I woke up, so to speak, and saw what a huge difference it did make. I saw it all one afternoon because of a game I had decided to play, because it was hot and because my bones were idle, and because there was something wrong in the house and I thought by playing this game I could somehow put it right. The game I invented was the game of imitating my father.

My father was a nice man but sometimes he'd drink too much whiskey and beat up my mom, and this made me so angry I wanted to kill him. But instead of killing him I decided to do something even better, which was to play this game. I found out where my dad hid his whiskey and I drank a whole bottle of it. Then I walked around in my underwear drunk, telling all the neighbors: "I'm drunk, just like my dad!"

They all laughed and thought I was a funny little eleven-year-old.

My mom came running after me and that's when the neighbors stopped thinking the game was funny—when I started yelling at my mom, since that's what my dad would have done and the game was to imitate my dad as much as I could.

"God damn bitch!" I yelled at my mom, who was flying around in circles in front of my face. "You're nothing but a whore bitch and I'm gonna make you pay!"

I remember my mom's face when I started playing this part of the game in front of the neighbors. The light went out of it like the sun going behind a cloud.

"Steven!" she shouted at me. "Stop it!"

But I went on with the game and started punching her with my little fists the way dad would have done, but it was hard because the ground was still spinning.

"I'm gonna make you pay," I said and cursed her the way my father would have cursed her. "You no good little slut, I'm gonna show you." Finally I felt my fist land in the soft part of her cheek.

My poor mom grabbed me by the hair and dragged me back home, and all the way I was shouting at her, even though I knew it was hurting her. I was drunk and I couldn't stop. I was kicking and screaming by the time she got me up to my room. Finally I got sick and threw up on my bed and only then was I able to stop playing the game.

"I'm sorry, Mom," I said.

I felt bad about the shadows on her face, and the way she looked at me—as if she didn't recognize her own son.

"You little fool!" she snapped. "In front of the neighbors!"

"I didn't mean it," I cried. "I'm sorry."

But that was the last time I really felt sorry for my mom because she did something then that she didn't have to do. After my dad came home from the fields she told him about it and I still don't see why she had to do that. She must have known what would happen.

I was lying up in my bed still feeling drunk and small as though I were rolling around inside a tin can when he came running into the room. His big green rubber boots coming toward the bed looked fourteen feet tall.

"Dad!" I cried. "What's wrong?"

He didn't explain. He grabbed me by the shirt and lifted me off the bed and threw me against the wall knocking the wind out of me. Then he threw me on the floor and ripped off my clothes and beat me all over my back and my butt with the buckle end of the belt, shouting things at me that I couldn't understand because he was like a monster now and he spoke in a monster language and the only thing I thought was "When is mom gonna come and stop him?" because every other time he'd beat me she had come in and said "Robert! That's enough!" and my dad had stopped.

"Mom!" I cried into the carpet as he whipped me.

"Mommy!"

But she didn't come and my dad kept whipping me until his son was dead, and that's when it didn't hurt any more. My dad had killed his own son, but it was okay because as he kept whipping the dead body I saw something deep inside myself, and it was a nice thing. It was a little patch of light inside me and I began talking to it.

"It's alright," I said to the little thing. "He can't hurt us."

The little thing glowed at me and we began skipping around together inside the dead body of my father's son, playing and singing together, and we didn't even notice when my dad finally stopped whipping the dead body and left the room.

The little patch of light had grown a smily freckled face just like my face, and curly red hair like my hair. He was wearing a checked shirt and nice blue shorts with little gray socks pulled all the way up to his tiny knees, just like what I usually wore, only a thousand times tinier. Since he was inside me it was hard to gauge, but his body could not have been more than a centimeter or two in height. He was the teeny tiniest, most magical little creature.

"Who are you?" I said, amazed.

"I'm your little boy," the thing said to me. "I'm Kevin."

"He didn't hurt you, did he, Kevin?" I asked the little boy.

"Just a bit," said the boy.

"I'll never let him hurt you again," I promised.

"And I'll never let him hurt you either, Dad," promised the boy, and we made a pact to stick together until the end of time, just me and my little boy.

The next morning I went down to breakfast to show my mom and dad that they didn't have a son any more.

"Have some eggs, Son," said my mom, trying to cheer me up.

"Okay," I said, eating the eggs like a little robot, staring straight ahead of me with no gleam in my eye so my parents would know their son was dead.

"You made a fool out of me in front of the neighbors," said my dad, trying to explain why he had beat me so hard.

"I'm sorry, Dad," I said, still staring with hollow eyes, and I said it like a dead boy who had no will of his own and just says it because he's supposed to. I could tell how much it hurt my father to listen to his dead son talking like that, who only yesterday had been alive and full of spunk. It made me feel good to hurt him.

And it made Kevin feel good, too. "Ha, ha," he was laughing inside. "Way to go, Dad!"

I took the dead Steven Jones's body to school and watched all the kids running around and having fun. Steven Jones couldn't play with them because he was dead. But a horrible question arose in my young mind. If I wasn't Steven Jones, who was I?

Since I couldn't play with the other children I had a lot of time to ponder this mystery. I spent the whole afternoon just sitting in the lunchroom, and just standing there during gym class, and just staring absently out from my desk in the back of the room, trying to make some sense of it all. By the end of the day I had come up with the following theory.

I had become two people at once. On the one hand I had become this little boy named Kev inside my head who had a tiny little face just like mine. And on the other hand I had become this guy who took care of Kev and who Kev called "Dad," who was invisible and had no face, but who had been freed of the false identity of Steven Jones by a severe thumping. And both of us were trapped inside Steven Jones's body. And both of us were the same person. When Kev looked at me, and I looked at Kev, it was like looking at my reflection in a puddle of water. But we were two different people.

"Dad," he grinned at me when I stared down at him.

"Kev."

In other words I was my own father.

"Steven," said Mrs. Rudder, the teacher, at the end of the day. "Is everything alright?"

"Yes," I squeaked.

I couldn't explain it to her because it was an impossible thing to explain. I couldn't even explain it to myself. I felt so confused with her looking at me as if she wanted to help that tears just started running out of my eyes. Then she hugged me and made me feel better.

"Mommy," I heard Kevin say, because he thought she was his mommy.

She smelled all flowery and felt so soft that it did seem possible for a second. She could have been Kevin's mommy. She wore such nice dresses and was such an impossibly nice teacher that she seemed the perfect mother for the impossible child. But then she took her hands off me and said "Oh no!"

I saw that there was blood on her hands from cuts on my back which were soaking through my shirt. I had been so busy trying to figure out the new state of affairs that I hadn't even noticed.

"I'm sorry," I said to her. She was so clean and flowery that I felt as though I was messing her up with the blood.

"What happened to you?" she asked, looking at her red hands.

"I fell off my bike."

"Oh." She peered into my eyes. "Have you been to a doctor?"

"My mom's taking me tonight," I lied, opening my eyes

wide and giving her the chance to see through my story and help me—maybe see Kevin in there at the bottom of that dark well—but she didn't, and that's when I realized that she wasn't Kevin's mom.

"Make sure you get that taken care of," was all she said. "It could get infected."

Kev was disappointed. That night in bed he asked me where his real mom was and I felt sorry for the little boy so I told him the story of how his mom had gotten lost and how we had come to this place to find her, and as soon as we found her we would go back.

"Go back where?" he asked me, and again I felt sorry, so I told him another story about the Impossible Land where everything was connected to everything else, just the way I was connected to Kev. In the Impossible Land nobody was alone or separate. Everyone was their own father and their own mother and everyone was a fish and everyone was a snake and everyone was everything.

"But what happened, Dad?" asked Kev.

I had to tell him the sad part about how we were all happy there, me and Kev and his mom, when one day by mistake his mom ate an apple with a worm in it and the worm was an evil worm. As soon as it got inside his mom the worm started to fly away.

9

"Help! Help!" cried his mom, but we couldn't do anything. The worm flew her up into the sky and into outer space and it took her here to Worm Land where everyone has an evil worm inside them and everyone is separate from everyone else.

"That's why we came here," I told him. "To find your real mom and bring her back."

"How did we get here?" he asked, and I told him that we built a Space Machine and flew here on it.

"Where's the Space Machine?" he asked. "I wanna go back now. I don't like it here."

"We can't go back yet," I said. "We have to find your mom."

Then I showed Kevin the peculiar thing about me which proved that my story was true. I took my clothes off in front of the mirror and I pointed to my belly.

"You see," I said. "I don't have a belly button."

A round balloon of belly was pushing out from my middle, and right at the spot where most people have the little gnarled hole called a belly button, the balloon remained perfectly smooth.

"You don't have one, either," I told him. "And that's because you don't have a worm."

I explained to Kevin that in Worm Land the worms live in people's belly buttons. If the person's belly button sticks out it means the worm is poking his head out. But if a person's belly button goes in, it means the worm is showing the world its butt.

"But where's the Space Machine?" he kept asking me, so I told him "We hid the Space Machine. We hid it so well that even we can't remember where it is, but as soon as we need it, we'll remember and we'll be able to find it."

For a while, though, whenever we saw a nice-looking girl Kevin would ask me "Is that Mom? Is that Mom?" and

I always had to say no.

This is a very important part of the story because later we're gonna get into all kinds of trouble because of the woman that really was Kevin's mom. But now I have to tell a different story.

RARE SHEEP

When I was about thirteen my dad went to the hospital and he learned how to stop drinking and he was like a different person after that. Me and Kev called him King Bob because of a story I made up about him.

We had to do something, because after he came back from the hospital my dad wanted to make everything better and he tried to be the nicest man on earth. He'd take my mom and I to the movies and he'd drive us all around the county in our station wagon and every Saturday he did something which made me and Kev feel awful.

He took us out, just me and Kev, not my mom, because he wanted to spend time with his son. He took me and Kev to the nicest restaurant in our town which served pancakes and all kinds of great food for breakfast. The sad thing was, he didn't realize that he didn't have his son with him and was wasting his time.

"Son," he'd say every Saturday morning at nine, after a knock at my bedroom door. "I'll go warm up the car."

My dad had this superstition that if he warmed up the station wagon for five minutes before he drove it the car would last longer. It was something about not flooding the valves, but when I looked at him sitting in there waiting for his car to warm up I had the feeling that it wasn't entirely necessary. I'd already seen how most people just got in their cars and drove off straight away. And I noticed that my dad was like that in his life, too. He'd never answer a question straight away like most people. He'd always pause for a moment, as though he was warming up his mind before answering, because of some other superstition he had.

"You can drive to my funeral in this station wagon," my dad would say. He really believed his superstition about warming up the car so I never questioned him about it.

Every Saturday morning he'd sit in his station wagon for five minutes, giving it a little gas every now and then, and I would hear him from my room. I always waited for the five minutes to pass before I went down. I didn't like just sitting in there with him doing nothing.

"Well," he'd say after I got in the car and we were heading off to town. "How's my son and heir?"

"Okay," I'd say.

Then he'd slap me on the knee affectionately and say, "That's a good feller."

At breakfast he'd sometimes tell me how big I was getting. I seemed to be growing fatter every week, but he always said "bigger."

"Pretty soon we'll have to let go of Lee Roy," he'd say.

Lee Roy was the boy who helped my dad on the farm.

"By the time you're fifteen," my dad would say, "poor Lee Roy will be out of a job. You'll be big enough to do all his work."

"Yeah."

One day at breakfast he said "How about we go into Grandville today and buy you some sheep?"

"Okay."

"When I was your age," he went on, "I had some of the rarest sheep you've ever seen. They had four horns, two going up and two going down, and they came from Africa.

I won first prize at the county fair. Ten dollars, which was a lot in those days."

"Wow."

"How would you like to raise some rare sheep?"

"Sure."

After breakfast he drove us all the way to Grandville and talked to a man in the market, and soon we were driving back with three rare sheep in the back of the station wagon making a terrible noise. (In all our excitement to get the rare sheep, we'd forgotten to bring a trailer.) But we got them home alright, three tiny sheep with short legs and thick wool which were called Soay sheep.

"They come from an island in the North Sea," my dad said. "That's the only place in the world where they raise 'em."

He showed me all kinds of things to do to make sure I'd win the prize in the county fair next spring. He showed me how to walk them around in a halter like little dogs so they wouldn't be scared when they had to do it in front of the judges. He showed me how to treat them with a solution if they got grubs in their wool, and how to keep their toes clipped and how to mix their special feed, which was supposed to make them fatter than the other sheep.

"Ha," laughed Kevin as we watched my dad walking back to the house that afternoon from the sheep field with his rubber boots and his plaid farmer's cap.

"What a jerk," Kevin said.

I felt horrible. My father was being so nice, but the person he was being nice to—his son—wasn't even there and hadn't been there for the two years since he'd been killed. And I could never be nice to him in return, because me and Kev had an agreement about hating him and making him pay for the rest of his life.

"Have you ever seen such a stupid jerk, Dad?" Kevin

asked as we watched my dad bending over to pull off his boots before he walked up on the back porch. Just before he went up, though, he looked back at me, across a hundred yards to the sheep field, and he smiled at me real quickly. Then he turned away and went into the house.

That night I went upstairs after dinner and told Kevin the story of King Bob. Kevin understood that it was a story about my father because my father's name was Robert and some of the farmers called him Bob.

KING BOB

King Bob was a king and he lived in ancient times when they rode on horses and fought battles with swords.

Kevin's little eyes grew all wide and I could tell he was really going to like the story.

King Bob was a great king but he didn't feel like a great king. He felt like a rotten king, even though he had a lot of sheep, because he didn't have a son. Every king needs a son to pass down his kingdom to, but King Bob had none. He had more sheep than any other king, sheep from all the foreign lands he had conquered, sheep from Denmark, Australia and China, but he still felt like a failure because he knew when he died the sheep would all die with him. That's what they did with kings who didn't have sons, they buried them in their own royal station wagons, and put all their sheep in there with them.

"Ah ha ha!" laughed Kevin. The more the story punished my father, the more Kevin seemed to like it. Soon I was laughing with him, even though I'd only told him the King Bob story in the first place to make him understand about my father.

The next night I told the story again, and made up more evil details. And the next night as I told Kevin the story I took out my whittling knife and began carving a piece of wood I'd found. Soon I'd carved the piece of wood into a little doll with a face that was square and had big grooves cut into it, and Kevin knew the doll was my father, because from years of drinking my father's face was full of crevices like that.

King Bob went to a one-eyed sorcerer in the woods and said "what is to become of my Kingdom?"

The one-eyed sorcerer said "King Bob, one day a red-haired boy with no head will bring down your kingdom and there is nothing you can do to prevent this misfortune."

"No way," said the king, storming home through the woods. "That sorcerer is a fool! How can you have red hair if you don't have a head?"

"Come on," he said to his right hand man when he got back to his castle. "Let's go invade somebody."

So King Bob and his right hand man, the Good Knight Steven, went off to fight a battle.

"Ah ha ha" yelped Kevin when I came up with the Good Knight Steven character. That was the biggest insult I had invented yet because every night after he watched the ten o'clock news and was ready for bed my father would knock on my door. He wouldn't open it, he'd just stand behind the closed door and call in "Good night, Steven."

I'd call back, "Good night, Dad," and me and Kev would kind of snicker to ourselves.

I'd picture him standing behind that door, afraid to come in and talk to me, and sometimes I'd feel sad and wish that my dad wasn't so afraid of me, because I didn't mean him any harm. But I didn't feel sad when I made up the Good Knight Steven character. I felt good because I was getting more and more sucked into the evil game every time I told

Kevin the King Bob story.

Soon the King Bob doll was all whittled and I painted a checkered crown on his head which matched the checkered cap my father and all the other farmers in my town wore. I painted baby blue royal robes which matched the baby blue windbreaker my father wore, and I gave the doll big green royal boots which matched my father's rubber boots.

Next to the king I placed another doll which represented the Good Knight Steven. To make it I used the color photograph of my face which had been taken that year in school. I wrapped the photo around the head of a GI Joe doll, which was about the same size as the King Bob doll. I sent them off to battle together on top of a toy car which I had bought at the hobby store. The toy car was a station wagon, but I had covered it with shiny glitter so it looked like the kind of car a king would drive in.

I would drive the toy station wagon all up and down my bed and around the floor of my room, and imagine with Kevin that they were fighting a great war against monsters and barbarians. Then I'd go on with the story.

Meanwhile, the Queen was praying to the angels every night while the king was off at war. She was praying "Please angels, please bring me a son so my husband won't have to be buried in his own station wagon."

The angels ignored her, but the Queen didn't lose faith. She prayed and prayed, because she was a good Queen, even though her face was covered with shadows from living with King Bob.

One night the angels heard the Queen's prayers, and they brought her a little magic boy from heaven, who was half man half angel. The baby boy had red hair because while the angels were flying with him down to earth, the little boy's hair had gotten burnt—they were moving so fast. But the Queen thought red hair was nice, since she hadn't heard about the sorcerer's warning. She said, "Thank you angels, you've brought me a beautiful boy with red hair."

The King returned victorious from his long battle, bringing back a truckload of sheep he had stolen from the barbarians.

"Bring in my son and heir," cried the King when he heard the news. "At last my no-good wife has given me a son. Jesus, Mary and Joseph it's about time."

They all gathered in the throne room for the royal inspection.

"Here is your son and heir," said the Queen proudly, showing him the baby.

The King was horrified.

"What's the matter, Robert?" asked the Queen.

The King looked at the baby, whose head was covered with little wisps of red. Then he remembered the words of the one-eyed sorcerer.

The King looked at the Good Knight Steven, whose head was covered with a green army helmet. Then he knocked off the Good Knight Steven's helmet with his sword.

"King Bob!" cried Steven. "What are you doing!"

Underneath the helmet was a big head of curly red hair.

"Traitor!" cried the King.

Then he turned to his wife.

"Slut!" he cried, thinking that she and the Good Knight had been messing around behind his back. "Now you must die!"

The king stuck his sword in his wife's heart.

"Oooo," she said, and she died.

Then the king went over to the baby and said, "No red-haired kid is going to take over my kingdom, especially not one born by that slut of a Queen!"

And he chopped off the baby's head.

"King Bob!" said the Good Knight Steven. "You've made a terrible mistake. I never touched your wife, I promise. She's not my type!"

"Suck on this," cried the King, and he stuck his sword in Steven's stomach and twisted it a few times until he had killed his right hand man.

But then the King looked down at the little baby whose head had rolled onto the floor, glowing in a strange way as though it was on fire. Then the little dead lips began to move.

"Why did you do this to me, Father?" said the baby in a sweet little voice. "I am sorry for you because now you will have to bear the burden of this hatred for the rest of your days.

"Ha ha!" said Kevin. "That's a good story, Dad!"

I thought it was a good story, too, and every night we worked out different variations with the story and our dolls.

I'd worked so hard on the King Bob doll he looked just like my father with his hands in his pockets, looking out into the distance like my father did when he was out in the fields during winter and nothing was growing.

Then I made a doll for the Dead Queen which looked like my mother, with shadows across her face and a stiff neck and the straight back of someone who never relaxed. Her clothes were polyester pants and shirts in sick green and orange colors that my mom bought from K-mart. But in the story those kinds of clothes were what the richest Queens and Princesses wore.

My story seemed to be going just right.

But in the daytime it didn't seem so good, because when my father would come back to the sheep field to see how I was doing with the Soays I wouldn't be able to talk to him the way he wanted me to talk to him. I'd just speak to him in short sentences: "Yes, Dad, uh uh, you're right." And when my dad walked away Kevin was even nastier about him.

"That jerk," he'd say. "He'll pay for the rest of his days for what he's done."

"No, Kev," I'd try to explain. "He didn't mean it."

"Yes he did, Dad," Kev would say. "He's mean."

"No, he's trying to make up for it..."

But Kevin didn't understand. And every time I told the King Bob story I would get confused too. So instead of telling it out loud to Kevin and using the dolls, I decided to work on the story by myself, on paper, drawing pictures to illustrate parts of it.

THE END OF
KING BOB

"**W**hy did you do this to me, Father," said the baby's head in a sweet little voice. "I am sorry for you because now you will have to bear the burden of this hatred for the rest of your days."

King Bob was scared. Suddenly the clouds darkened and the wind started whipping up. Some lightning cracked. Hail and sleet poured from the heavens. The animals all ran for cover and people bolted up the doors of their houses and King Bob knew he'd messed up. Standing there over his victims the words of the dead baby were echoing in his mind: "You will bear the burden of this hatred for the rest of your days."

Soon he heard a mob outside the castle. The people had heard that King Bob had done an evil thing which had loosed a plague upon the land and now they wanted to make him pay.

"Kill the king! Kill the king!" they cried, as they began burning down the castle and murdering all the King's sheep.

"There he is!" the people shouted, breaking into the throne room.

"Kill him! Kill him!" they screamed. "He brought this gloom upon us!"

Luckily, King Bob ducked into a secret passageway in the fireplace of the throne room and escaped.

"Aren't the people even gonna chase him through the secret passageway, Dad?"

"No," I said. "They don't know about the secret passageway."

"That's not fair, Dad," he said.

"Be quiet, Kevin," I said, and I went on with the story.

King Bob followed the secret passageway underground through the castle and under the moat, finally ending up way in the middle of the woods. Standing in front of him was the one-eyed sorcerer.

"Help me! Help me!" begged King Bob. "I have to find the soul of the red-haired boy and bring it back!"

"That's impossible," said the one-eyed sorcerer. "The red-haired boy is dead."

"Fool!" cried King Bob, and he stuck his sword into the sorcerer's one eye and killed him.

"I'll find the red-haired boy," he said. "I don't care what you say. I will go to the Land of the Dead and bring him back."

King Bob wandered around some more, searching for the Land of the Dead, but he couldn't find it. No matter where he went, everything around him was alive.

"Where is the Land of the Dead?" he asked the birds, but the birds shrugged their shoulders.

"We don't know," they said.
"Do you know where the Land of the Dead is?" he asked a bear.

This was depressing for King Bob. All the creatures of the earth had become atheists.

"Isn't there another world beyond ours?" he asked a tree.

"This can't be true!" cried King Bob, while in his ears echoed the words of the red-haired boy.

Then it hit King Bob.
"Eureka!" he cried. "I know where the Land of the Dead is. The Land of the Dead is in... death! I have to kill myself!"

King Bob took out his sword and stuck it in his ear. Blood came trickling out of his mouth and ears. And he died.

"Okay, Kev," I said when I killed King Bob in the story. "I guess it's time for bed."

"Is that it?" said Kev.

"Well, that's it for now," I said. "I'm tired."

"Oh," said Kev, and I could tell by the look on his face that something was going on in his little head.

"I thought you didn't like King Bob," I said when I got into bed.

"I don't like him," said Kev.

The next night I continued the story.

Kevin looked different. For the first time since I'd known him he seemed scared of something. I didn't know what it was. But I decided to go on with the story, even though the main character was dead.

King Bob died and entered the Land of the Dead. It looked

exactly like the Land of Life. There were birds and bears and trees. But no red-haired boy with no head. King Bob searched everywhere, wandering around with his sword still stuck in his ear, but he couldn't find him.

"I guess he's not here," said King Bob. "I might as well go back to the Land of Life."

He pulled the sword out of his ear and expected to be transported back to the land of life, but nothing happened.

Then a horrible thought occurred to him.

"Maybe I'm stuck here forever, now that I'm dead!"

He asked the birds how one could get back to the Land of Life.

He asked the bear.

He asked the tree.

Then King Bob came to a kingdom. He asked everyone he met in the kingdom if they could tell him how to get back to the Land of Life, or if they'd seen a red-haired boy with no head. People thought he was crazy. And nobody would speak to him until he met an old blind woman who looked like a witch.

"Psst," whispered the old woman. "Psst. Psst."

"What?"

"I know the boy you're talking about—the red-haired boy with no head."

"Where is he?" cried King Bob, getting all excited.

The old woman leaned over to whisper nervously: "A red-haired boy with no head came to this very kingdom not long before you did."

"That's him! That's him!"

"He came to this kingdom, but he didn't stay long."

"Where did he go?"

"He went south," whispered the old lady close to King Bob's face, and her breath smelled like a refrigerator that needed to be cleaned.

"South? Which way is south?"

The old blind woman pointed to the ground.

"Down below," she said.

King Bob got scared, and started shaking, but he knew he had to do it, so he asked the witch how to get down below.

"You may never come back," warned the witch.

"I must go," insisted King Bob.

"Then I'll show you."

The witch took King Bob to a place on the outskirts of the kingdom where there was a little shack.

"What's that?" asked King Bob.

"The elevator."

The witch pushed the button and they waited for the elevator to come.

"It's bleak out here," said King Bob, because out there on the outskirts of the kingdom everything was flat and dusty and the wind made a whistling sound.

"It's bleaker down there," she said. And they waited in silence some more.

"Sure is taking a long time for the elevator to come, said King Bob.

"It's a slow elevator," said the witch, and they waited some more.

"It's a bad elevator," said Kevin. "Don't make him go down below, Dad, please."

"But that's where the red-haired boy is," I explained, "and King Bob has to find him."

"No!" Kevin snapped. "I'm not going down there!"

Finally the elevator came.

"Jesus, Mary and Joseph, it's about time," said King Bob.

The doors opened and King Bob looked inside a tiny little box.

"It's a long way down," said the witch, pointing to the ground.

"How far down is it?" King Bob asked, but then he knew the answer without having to hear it.

"I know, I know," he said. "It's as far as I can imagine."

"No," said the witch. "It's further than you can imagine. It's further than infinity itself!"

"I don't care," said the King, and he stepped inside the box. On the wall of the elevator were some buttons, and they looked like this:

A billion trillion miles ●

Infinity ●

Further than infinity ●

A lot further than infinity ●

Down Below ●

He pushed the button that said Down Below, and as the elevator door started closing he heard the witch beginning to snicker in a horrible, evil way.

"I'll be waiting here when you come back," she laughed. "If you come back... ah ha ha ha ha!"

It was too late for King Bob to change his mind. Just before the doors closed he saw the old woman ripping off her face, as though her face was made of plastic. And behind this plastic face King Bob saw her real face, and he recognized it! It was a man's face, a face with one eye, which didn't even work because someone had poked a hole in it. It was the one-eyed sorcerer in disguise!

(I'd already explained to Kevin that the sorcerer had only one eye because a whiskey bottle only has one eye. Now I explained that the elevator the sorcerer sent King Bob into was like the hospital that my dad got sent to because of whiskey.

The sorcerer at the top of the elevator was laughing at my dad because even though my dad had gotten cured of drinking, it was still somewhere in his eyes when you looked at him, the desire to get drunk and act like an animal and beat everybody up.)

"Have a nice trip, King Bob," cried the sorcerer. "Oh! sweet revenge! Ah ha ha!"

King Bob tried to rush out but the doors closed too fast. He'd been tricked, and now he was stuck in a box that was so small that he couldn't stand up straight, and he couldn't sit down either. He had to hunch over in the most uncomfortable position he could imagine. And he felt the box sinking deep into the earth.

"Help me!" he cried. "This is horrible!"

Then he noticed the elevator music, which was a horrible

annoying melody going on and on and never changing.

"Oh God," he said, "where's that horrible music coming from?"

He searched all around but he couldn't find a speaker and he decided that the music was coming from inside his own brain so he banged his head against the walls. But the music didn't stop, it just got more annoying, as the elevator descended at a snail's pace. King Bob stood there aching, hunched over in the tiny box. And he had plenty of time to think about all his sins.

"I'm sorry," he said. "I shouldn't have killed my wife, or my right hand man, or the red-haired boy with no head. I shouldn't have been so selfish and mean!"

But it didn't do him any good. Days and days passed. He tried to fall asleep, but the music and his awkward position made it impossible.

"Shut up! Shut up!" he would scream.

The elevator hardly seemed to be moving at all, and finally King Bob gave up all hope.

"This is the most horrible torture imaginable. And it's going to go on and on for the rest of time. And I'm going to suffer... and suffer... and suffer."

Tears came out of his eyes. Only then did the elevator door open.

"At last!" he cried. And he jumped out into the open. It felt so good to stand up straight. "Oooh," he said, stretching his arms and legs. "Ahhh, that's so much better. Thank you, God. Thank you!"

Then he noticed where he was.

What he saw is hard to describe. There wasn't anything there, but the place wasn't empty. If you say a place is empty, then there is something that has been emptied out; first it was full and now it is empty. But there wasn't anything in this place which could have been emptied out. It was the Place Without Space!

EMPTY   MORE THAN EMPTY

When King Bob looked ahead of him he didn't see anything at all. He didn't see pitch black. He didn't see blinding light. He didn't see a huge empty space. He didn't see anything.

But he heard a voice. Ahead of him in the Place Without Space there was a voice calling "King Bob, King Bob."

It was the voice of the red-haired boy with no head.

"Hooray!" cried King Bob. "I've found him!"

King Bob started running toward the Place Without Space, but the problem was that King Bob himself took up space, so he could never get into the Place Without Space. He ran and ran but he never came to it. It went around him and it stayed in front of him and it went behind him and King Bob was trapped there forever trying to get in and trying to get out. And his punishment was never finished, and he never found any relief, not even in death, since he had already died a long time ago. Throughout all eternity his only hope was that voice, which he never could catch up to, even though he chased it forever, like a dog chasing his tail.

    "Poor King Bob," Kevin said when I finished writing the story.
    I went over and I looked at the little wooden doll we called King Bob, who was stuck forever in a place lonelier than Hell.

"Isn't there anything we can do for him, Dad," Kevin asked.

"Well," I said, "we can try to be as nice as we can to him, because he's suffered enough already."

The next day when we watched my dad walking around in the fields I heard Kevin saying it again.

"Poor King Bob," he said, and then I knew the story had worked. Kevin had understood the we lived in a place that my father could never get to, and that it made my father suffer, and there was no reason for us to add to his suffering.

At night me and Kev would still play with the dolls.

"The doll of the angel," I'd tell Kevin, "is just like the spaceship that we came in from the Impossible Land."

"That's why we have red hair," Kevin would say.

"That's right, Kev," I'd say.

The last doll in the story, the red-haired boy with no head, was the only doll which wasn't made out of beechwood. This doll was made out of nothing and you just had to imagine it, because it was impossible to make a doll that had red hair and no head at the same time. So this was the invisible doll, and we imagined that even though it had no head it had red hair, and it had two faces, one on the front and one on the back, and no belly button, and it was its own father, just like me and Kev, and it broke all the laws of logic. It was the Impossible Child.

We made other dolls, too, for other stories, and our favorite doll of all was the doll of Kevin's real mother, not the Dead Queen, but a beautiful woman who also had red hair from when the worm flew her away to the Impossible Land. She had big eyes like rubies, which we showed by gluing in some red stones that we found in my mother's jewelry box. We put some perfume on her, too, and made her smell like flowers, and we sewed a little dress and covered it with glitter and made her all sparkly, and we gave her nice breasts with nipples sticking out too because that made me excited, and sometimes I imagined doing sex things with that doll whose name I imagined was Mara.

"Da-ad," Kevin would say when he caught me imagining dirty things with the Mara doll, and he'd put his one hand over his eyes as if he couldn't bear looking at me while I was thinking of such things.

Sometimes he wanted to do something with the Mara doll, though, which was pretty strange, too, and I wouldn't allow it. He wanted to imagine that he was sucking on one of the nipples we had given her, not like a sex thing, but he wanted to imagine that there was milk in there, and that he was her little baby. I would tell him "No, Kevin, you're too old," and if he kept bugging her I would imagine that the Mara doll spanked him on the behind and made Kevin cry, but it was all just a game and we were having fun.

From playing these games with the dolls and learning the story of King Bob I was able to become best pals with my dad before too long. Every Saturday my dad would take me out to breakfast as usual, but it seemed we were having more fun every week, talking in longer sentences and getting more comfortable with each other. Afterwards I'd show him the sheep and all the things I'd been doing to make them the best sheep and he was really sure that I would win a prize when the county fair came around next summer.

That's how I learned the language of sheep, from spending so much time out there in the field with the three Soays my dad had bought me and the hundred or so other regular sheep that he kept.

THE LANGUAGE OF SHEEP

At first it didn't make any sense to me, all the noise the sheep made. But the more time I spent with them the more I noticed that they had different ways of making noise for different things they were trying to say. Sometimes they did the regular kind of bleating which sounded like *baah*. But other times they made a higher-pitched sound, *beeh*. And once in a while you'd think they were about to throw up because it sounded like *blaaah!* Or like they were going to die because they sounded so sad, like *waaah, waaah*. But even though I had a sense of it, I couldn't figure out exactly what any of these sounds meant, because I was still thinking in the language of worms.

Worms inside humans are mainly interested in keeping separate from each other and their language helps them with this, because it's based on something I knew from English class was called "pronouns." A pronoun tells which worm you are speaking about in a sentence. If you're talking about the worm inside yourself you say "I." If you're talking about the worm in front of you, you say "you." If you're talking about the worm down the street you say "he-she-it." If you're talking about all the separate worms you say "we worms." Finally, there's a pronoun for

35

the worms that are not only separate from you but rotten and you don't like them—the "they" or "them worms."

The thing with sheep, I noticed, was that they didn't have worms in them. I saw that from the way they always stayed together in groups and from the way they all looked as if they were going through the same thing out there in the field. There wasn't a single sheep that was doing anything different from being a sheep. Even the three rare sheep that we thought were so special—they had no idea they were rare sheep! They just mixed up with the ordinary sheep like brothers. And when sheep talked, I noticed, they weren't using pronouns, and that was the first difference between their language and worm-language.

There was another difference between worm language and theirs, and that was: when we talk, the person we're talking to has to wait for us to finish before it's his turn to speak—that's only polite. But it's not the way the sheep talk. They all talk at the same time, and nobody waits for anybody to finish what they're saying. They all talk at once. It's like they're one big sheep orchestra playing a horrible-sounding music, because there's no conductor and no music to follow and everyone just makes whatever noise they feel like making at the time.

It sounded horrible to me at first, anyhow. But one day while I was out there tending to my Soays, one of them started off the concert by going *baah*, and it sounded so sweet that somehow I knew what he was saying, just from his sad, sweet way of looking when he said it. He was saying "lonely." Not "I'm lonely," but just "lonely." That's the way I translated his sheep word. Then another one went *waaah* and I knew what he was saying too! He was saying "scared, scared." A third one joined in the singing then, saying *baah waaah*, and I noticed he was imitating the first two sheep and what he was saying meant "lonely and scared."

Soon, as the whole flock was going *baah waaah,* saying "lonely and scared," I saw one of them wandering off, bleating *maaaha* and I knew what he meant from the panic in his voice. He meant "lost!" The rest of them heard this and stopped saying what they were saying and started going "lost, lost," just like him, and they all went over to huddle around the lost sheep to make him feel connected again.

Yeaaah! I heard someone cry suddenly, and I noticed a sheep in the corner of the field sounding overjoyed because he had found a patch of fresh clover, so I knew he meant "real good eating over here!" The rest of the sheep charged over there where the grass was darker and they were all saying *yeaaaha, yeah,* "real good eating," so I figured I'd go over there too to observe some more. But when I went over there they all looked at me with beady eyes and shouted *Aaaaa!*—"danger coming, danger!"

I didn't want them to be afraid of me, so I got down on my knees and I started eating the clover and pretending to be a sheep, saying it just like they said it, *yeah,* "real good eating." Soon they stopped shouting "danger" at me and went back to saying "real good eating," and I stayed down there for a long time chewing up the grass.

As I chewed and they accepted me into their company, I began to feel connected to the sheep just like I was connected to Kevin and it was wonderful. A bunch of sheep together in a field, I realized, thinks its just one great big thing, all connected, and the reason they talk is to keep the connection going. It seemed exactly the opposite of why people talk, which is to make sure there is no connection and that the other person realizes that he or she is a separate worm. "I like this," one person will say, and the other person will answer, "I like that." "It's my opinion," one person will declare, and the other person will counter,

"Well, I disagree." And that's the way all the worms manage to keep themselves apart, but down there with the sheep just like with Kevin I had discovered a way of talking that connected me with other beings and those sheep became the first friends besides Kevin that I ever had.

They were suspicious of me, of course. Every time I showed up in the field they greeted me with that nasty *aaah!*—"danger danger." But one day I took some wool that was in the barn from last year's shearing and made myself a sheep costume. I took off all my clothes and slipped into the wool, and I went crawling out onto the field.

"Woooo," they said. "Woooo."

I didn't know what that meant, but it sounded nicer than "danger danger," and the sheep let me hang out with them all afternoon. I did my best to convince them I wasn't separate. I ate tons of clover, which made me puke, but I wasn't embarrassed about puking in front of them—that would have given it away.

Another thing I couldn't be embarrassed about was pooing in front of them, because the sheep loved pooing and even had a special word for it because it made them feel so good. *Mmmm* they would say after they'd finished. "That was nice big poo and it felt goo-ood." So I pooed out there and it got on my legs, but I went *Mmmm* and all the other sheep went *Mmmm*, "nice big poo," even though a few of them said *Woooo* again and I still didn't know what that word meant.

Afterwards, when I went back to the barn to clean up and put on my clothes, I started to get worried about whether my mother or father, or maybe a neighbor, had seen me out there naked with wool around my body, pooing in the field with the sheep.

"They'll think you're crazy," Kev warned me.

"You're right," I said. "I've got to be more careful."

It wasn't until about a week later, when my mom had gone out shopping and my dad was way out in the fields, that I dared to put on the sheep outfit again. I went out there and was pretending to be a sheep when something strange happened. One of the sheep came over and started acting all friendly like I'd never seen a sheep act before. Even though they're not separate from each other, sheep are never too friendly, either. I guess it's because they don't have to show it, they know they're all best pals. But this afternoon this one sheep was getting all affectionate and rubbing his face in mine, and saying that strange word I still hadn't figured out yet: *wooo, woooo.* I looked at the sheep and then I looked between the legs of the other sheep and realized my stupid mistake. First of all it wasn't *his* face that was rubbing against mine, it was *her* face. All the sheep were girls! We only brought in male sheep once a year for lambing. Even the Soays were ewes, but for some reason all this time I'd been thinking about them as boys, like me.

Then I saw it hanging down underneath me—the thing that made me not a girl—and I realized all the sheep could see it too. They all knew I was a boy!

"Wooo," the sheep said as she rubbed her face against mine. *"Wooo, woooo."*

I knew then what the sheep wanted me to do.

"Don't do it, Dad," said Kevin. "You'll get in trouble."

"Wooo," said the sheep. *"Woooooo."*

"No, Dad!" cried Kevin.

I tried to show the sheep that I didn't feel like doing it, but I couldn't think of the right word.

"Naaah," I bleated at her. *"Naaaaaah."*

The sheep looked up at me and said, *"Haaaaa?"* with a quizzical look on her face.

"Naaah," I said again.

The other sheep began getting suspicious and they came over to see what I was doing. They said some more things that I didn't understand, looking at me with beady eyes as though they were mad at me.

"Woooooo," said the girl sheep and started turning herself around in front of me, waiting. I felt as though I had to do it then, otherwise my weeks of convincing the sheep to be my friend would be wasted.

"Dad," cried Kevin, putting his hand over his face so he wouldn't see me trying to do what the girl sheep wanted me to do.

"I have to do it, Kev," I said.

Then it happened. Just as I came behind the sheep and started trying to find how to do what she wanted me to do, and while the girl sheep was making all kinds of sounds that I had never heard before, I heard another sound and I didn't know what it meant because I was so into the sheep way of talking. But Kevin was going "Dad! Dad!" trying to get me to listen.

Suddenly I recognized the high-pitched voice. My mother was shouting at me from the fence.

"Steven!" she was crying. "Steven!"

"Oh no," I said, rolling off the sheep. I saw my mom over there with a bag of groceries, more shadows on her face than ever before.

"Oh, Mom," I said, lying there on my back ashamed of myself.

It was too much for her. She started bawling and ran away to the house, groceries falling out of her bag on the way.

"It's okay, Dad," said Kevin. "It's okay."

I heard the sheep. They were all yelling *waaah, aaah,* and they had run clear over to the other end of the field, glaring at me as if I were some kind of fake.

I didn't even try to make it up to them. I knew I had lost my first friends. Instead I walked back to the barn and cleaned myself up and slowly dressed. I was afraid to go in the house so I walked all the way into town, then up into the woods, where I found a pond, which I found out later was called "Shepherd's Pond," which seems funny to me now, seeing how I first went there after being such a shepherd, but there weren't any sheep up at this pond. There wasn't anything except a little green pond and some frogs jumping around and some birds tweeting. It was real quiet and it was a good place to be, so I stayed there just looking into the pond for hours and hours until it went dark.

On the way back through town I asked the man at the liquor store to sell me a small bottle of whiskey, telling him my mother had a cold. He let me have it since he knew my mom, and before I went home I put a little in my mouth.

"Mom," I said when I saw her in the kitchen, covered in darkness, staring blankly at the table, which was covered with a blue plastic tablecloth with white flowers on it. She seemed lost somewhere in that pattern of flowers and hardly noticed me come in.

"Mom, I didn't know what I was doing. I was drunk."

"Oh, Steven," she said, not looking up. "Steven, Steven."

"I'm sorry, Mom," I said. "I'll never do it again."

I don't know if she believed my story. The next day I didn't care because she had done something that she didn't have to do—again! I knew it right away when I came home from school and something seemed funny about the place, something seemed missing. I walked out back and there it was, the sheep field, as empty as the Place Without Space. Then I knew my mom had told on me—again! Why else would my dad have taken the day off work and driven all the sheep into Grandville and sold every one of them, even the three rare ones, spoiling all our plans for the county fair? Why else if he hadn't heard the whole Disgusting Story?

GOOD GUY

Next Saturday when my dad knocked on my door as usual I didn't ask about the sheep. He had become such a good guy since being in the hospital that even the Disgusting Story wasn't going to stop him from having his dead son back. He still wanted to go to Deason's for breakfast.

"I'll be down in a minute," I said, and he went down to warm up the car.

We went driving to town as usual, and he said, as usual, "How's my son and heir," but it didn't sound the same. It sounded fake, as if even my dad was getting tired of the game of pretending he had a son.

While we were sitting in Deason's I watched him eating his eggs and bacon, concentrating too hard on cutting the toast and looking around the restaurant and doing anything he could think of to keep from looking at me. This was even worse than before, when he liked me but I didn't like him. Now we didn't like each other and we both were glad when breakfast was over and we could go home and hide.

The next Saturday when he knocked on my door I said "No, Dad, I don't feel like going today."

"What?" he said, opening the door and looking at me as though I'd hurt his feelings.

"Maybe next week," I said.

"Okay, fine," he said, nodding his head and grunting something I couldn't hear as he closed the door.

After that he didn't knock on my door on Saturdays. He didn't ask me to help him in the fields, either. And when I turned fifteen it didn't happen the way he said it was going to: Lee Roy didn't lose his job and I didn't take over his duties.

My dad was still just like King Bob, with a whole kingdom and no son to hand it over to. Late at night me and Kev would talk to the King Bob doll.

"It's okay, King Bob," we'd say. "You don't have to keep searching for the red-haired boy, 'cause guess what? The Dead Queen has just given birth to another boy and this is a boy without red hair! Your very own son and heir! You'll like him so much, 'cause he wants to be just like you and he wants you to take him to Deason's and he's a good guy. That's his name, even: Good Guy."

I made a carving of a guy named Good Guy who did all the things he was supposed to do in school. He came running home afterward to King Bob and said, "Hey Pop, I'm home," and they slapped hands together and went out to the fields where King Bob taught him how to sow different types of grain and how to lay split rail fences and how to build electric fences and how to spread silage and how to bale hay and how to drive a combine and Good Guy loved it and King Bob loved Good Guy and everything was great.

But the Dead Queen was not happy. She was dead and she didn't like her husband. She didn't seem to like anything all that much—she just put up with it, and that's why she stood up so straight and tall, and spoke with a high-pitched voice, because even though she didn't like any of it she was surviving, and that made her proud, but not happy.

So sometimes we did something especially nice to the Dead Queen, which was to bring her back to the Land of Life. Not the part of the Land of Life when she was messed up with mean old King Bob. We brought her way back in time, long before King Bob killed her, before they even got married, when she was a princess in a far away land and she used to ride on elephants with her brothers and everything was great.

We carved some elephants and we took the Dead Queen riding around our bedroom on them, and she was happy and everyone loved her in the far away land, and she didn't have any shadows on her face either because we'd painted her face bright again in the colors of the rainbow, and she laughed and jumped up and down on top of her elephant. It made me and Kev so happy to see her having fun that we cried sometimes.

In the end, though, we always had to bring her back to the Land of the Dead. And even though we promised her we'd let her ride elephants again the next time we played, shadows always came back into her face and me and Kev felt sad. We couldn't bear looking at her so we'd put that doll under the bed before we went to sleep.

Going to sleep was the strangest time of all because Kevin didn't sleep, he just watched me. I'll explain more about that later, but the next part of the story is not about that. The next part of the story is about going to school.

SCHOOL

I used to go to school in sloppy clothes with my shirt not tucked in and I never brushed my hair either because I wasn't Steven Jones. I was the Invisible Father of the Impossible Child inside him, and I didn't care how Steven Jones looked. The other kids dressed up in nice clothes and spent their time trying to be the most popular kid or the funniest kid or the smartest kid and I didn't fit in with them.

They made fun of me sometimes because of the way I looked. "Steven the Blob," they called me. "Here comes Steven the Blob."

"Why are you so fat," Kevin asked me one day as we got on the bus, after some kids had been calling me Steven the Blob and Fatso and Piece of Shit.

"Because," I explained, holding up my rolls of fat in the mirror. "This way nobody can tell that I don't have a belly button."

When I pressed the fat together on my stomach it formed a cleft that easily passed for a belly button.

"This way, if we ever get caught," I continued, "we can fake having one."

In addition to being fat I smelled bad. I didn't wash much because me and Kev stayed perfectly clean inside

Steven Jones and it was boring to stand there in the shower. My shoelaces, too, remained untied most of the time because I got out of breath bending down to tie them. And maybe if I'd been paying more attention I would have noticed other things: my fly undone, my shirt buttoned lop-sidedly, pizza on my face. But I didn't notice any of these things because I was deeply involved in a research project.

I spent all my time in the library reading books, trying to find out if there were other people like me and Kev on the planet who felt like an Impossible Child stuck in the Land of Worms. I went to a lot of movies, too. And sometimes I'd find a story that was almost talking about what I was going through, and I'd get excited, but always when the story ended I'd be disappointed.

"No, they weren't talking about me," I'd think, coming out of the movie, or putting the book down. "They were almost talking about me, but not quite."

The idea came to me to write a story about being me, just in case there were any others out there. Sometimes I thought there might be thousands of us out there, and it was all a conspiracy of the worms to keep us quiet so we never found out about each other. But other times I felt like me and Kev were all alone on the planet and everyone else was a worm and nobody would understand what I was writing. But I kept at it, even if it was a waste of time. I worked on it all day and night, and sometimes I'd get a whole bunch of pages written and throw them all out and start over. I wanted it to be perfect, so that someone could read it and understand exactly who I was.

The more I worked on the story, though, the worse I did on my exams in school. I had stopped paying attention to the teachers, so hard was I concentrating on my story, and come report card time I had failed everything, so I ran home and got the report cards out of the mail so my parents wouldn't find out. I changed all the Fs to As and even added a comment on the bottom saying "Steven is doing brilliantly in school and is very popular with the other children. No need to worry."

"Ha ha!" laughed Kevin. "They'll never know!"

My parents were happy, but the story wasn't coming so good. By the time the next report card came I had failed again, and had to rip up a special letter they sent home asking for a conference.

By the end of the year, though, the story was finished and I was happy with it. It was called The Destruction of the Worm.

THE DESTRUCTION
OF THE WORM

Neville was born April 31st and that explained why his parents never gave him a birthday party. It also explained why he didn't have a worm inside him.

"Maybe April 31st will come next year," said his parents. "And we'll give you a big birthday party."

But next year April 31st didn't come. April 30th led straight into May 1st and the poor boy's birthday was forgotten. He didn't mind so much. What bothered him was not having a worm in his belly like everyone else in the kingdom. Everyone in the kingdom had a belly button that either poked in or out, depending on which way the worm in there was looking. But Neville had a smooth belly and he didn't know what to do with himself.

The worms in the kingdom, you see, told the people what to do. If it was a young worm the people knew they were young and they went to school. If it was an old worm the people knew they were old so they went to old folks homes. If it was white they lived in white houses. If it was black they lived in black houses. And if it was a boy worm the people looked for girls so they could lie down on top of them and let the boy worm touch the girl worm through their bellies. And if it was a powerful worm the people lived in the castle with the most power of all, the Emperor, who had a huge belly button that stuck out almost two feet—that's how the people knew he was their Emperor. And that's how everyone knew exactly who they were.

Not Neville, though—poor Neville. When people asked Neville what he was doing, Neville didn't have an answer, and he was confused.

"Where is my worm," the boy wondered. "Maybe this year April 31st will come and I'll figure out what I'm supposed to do."

But his birthday didn't come and finally the boy couldn't stand it any more, he decided to take decisive action.

"I will eat a worm," he said.

He went into the garden and gobbled up an earthworm. But the worm got digested in his stomach and came out in his poo, dead. It wasn't the right worm.

"Where is the right worm?' Neville wondered.

He went searching throughout the kingdom with little Petri dishes and he gathered up 33 varieties of worm—some red and some purple and some long and some short, and even some with tiny legs scampering along the ground. He ate a worm of each variety, one by one, but they all came out in his poo.

"Damn!" Neville said, now more confused than ever.

By this time he had learned a lot about worms and had enough information to concoct a special potion.

"If I can't join 'em," he thought to himself, "I'll beat 'em!"
This potion he invented was supposed to dissolve the worms inside everyone in the kingdom and then, Neville thought,

everyone would be just like him—confused—and every day would be April 31st. Neville took this potion up into the hills and he poured it into the big reservoir which was the water supply for the entire kingdom.

Soon strange things started happening in the kingdom. The more water they drank, the less sure of themselves the people became. The Emperor himself was affected. In the middle of a speech he forgot why he was talking.

"I'm sorry," said the Emperor to the hushed and embarrassed crowd. "What was I saying?"

Neville noticed the Emperor's belly button had shrunk to about three inches where it protruded from his belly.

Soon everybody in the kingdom felt dizzy. The baker forgot why he was baking the bread and let it all burn in the ovens. The butcher forgot why he was carving the meat and let it go rotten in the store. The candlestick maker stopped making candlesticks and everything went dark in the kingdom. The mothers stopped being mothers. The fathers stopped being fathers. Everyone was wandering around aimlessly with the same expression on their faces.

"It's April 31st!" Neville cried. "Don't worry, you'll get used to it after a while."

"Oh," said the people, scratching their heads. "Why did you do this to us? We were happy knowing who we were."

"No," explained Neville. "This is much better. We're all the same now. Everyone is just a person, no different from anyone else."

"Oh," the people said, but in a little while everything was messed up in the kingdom. Old people were acting like babies, playing silly games, or trying to go to school, thinking they were young. Young people were limping around in the old folks homes. And boys started getting on top of other boys and pressing their bellies together. And girls did the same with girls. White people went into black people's houses and black people went into white people's houses, and everything was mixed up.

Then a noise was heard outside the kingdom. Horses were approaching and cannons were firing off. The Enemy was invading!

The people ran to the Emperor.

"The Enemy is invading!" they cried. "What should we do!"

Neville noticed the Emperor's belly button again. It had shriveled up into nothing at all.

"Er," the Emperor muttered, taking off his crown. "What's this thing doing on my head?"

The Enemy broke through the walls of the kingdom and rounded up all the people, saying "Ha! Now we're in control and you will do only what we tell you!"

"Yay!" cried the people, and the Enemy was confused by this happy reaction.

"At last," the people cried, kissing the Enemy's feet. "Someone will tell us what to do!"

"Hmmm," went the Enemy commander to his next in command. "This has all been too easy. It must be some sort of trick. We'll have to exterminate them all before it's too late."

"You will all line up in front of the cathedral," instructed the Enemy soldiers.

"Yay," cried the people. "We will all line up in front of the cathedral!"

Neville peeked into the cathedral and saw a truck in the back filling the whole place up with a poisonous gas.

"I have to save the village," thought Neville.

He went to the Enemy soldiers with a jug of water from the reservoir.

"Aren't you thirsty, Enemy soldiers?" Neville asked. "Here, drink some water."

The Enemy soldiers drank the water and soon the worms inside them started dissolving.

"The people are all lined up," the soldiers said to the Enemy commander. "Who should we kill first?"

The Enemy commander scratched his head.

"Er... " he said. "What was the question?"

Neville ran home and made an antidote to the poison and poured it into another jug, which he gave to all the villagers, and soon the worms inside the villagers started growing back, as the Enemy soldiers all wandered about scratching their heads.

"What's going on here," cried the Emperor, and Neville saw a three-inch worm protruding from his royal girth. "Arrest these men."

The villagers rounded up the confused Enemy soldiers and they became slaves of the Emperor.

"The cathedral is full of poison," explained Neville. "They were going to exterminate the village!"

"Yay," the people cried when they saw how they had been saved by the young boy. "You're our hero," they said.

The Emperor gave Neville a medal and they had a big parade, making the Enemy soldiers drag around big floats. And now they have a holiday in the kingdom commemorating Neville's birthday, April 31st, the special day they added to the calendar, and it is everybody's favorite holiday because on that day everybody forgets what their job is and who they are, and they go crazy, marching around with burnt bread, which is a reminder of how the baker burnt the bread, and everything is dark on this holiday, which is a reminder of how the candlestick maker forgot to make the candlesticks, and all the meat is let out to go rotten, which is a reminder of how the butcher forgot to butcher the meat. And finally, whoever is the Emperor at the time has to walk around holding his crown saying "What's this thing doing on my head?" and all the people laugh and sing and remember the boy with no belly button who didn't have a birthday and didn't have a worm.

I read the story to Kevin and he thought it was a good story.

"Let's have a parade, Dad," he said, so we made some little dolls to represent the characters and we marched around the room pretending it was April 31st, and it was so much fun that I decided to show my story to the English teacher, who knew a lot about books. I thought maybe he could help me get it published.

THE TALK

A few days after I gave the English teacher the story I got a note that said I had to go to the principal's office. When I got to the principal's office I saw a man sitting in his overalls looking very upset—my father! And next to him was a woman, with her lips all pursed—my mother. And both of them looked as though someone had died.

"Sit down, Steven," said the principal. "This is Dr. Ciccone from the board. I've called him in here to have a talk with you and your parents. You don't mind do you?"

"No," I said.

The "talk" was a bunch of questions from the doctor, a man with thick-lensed glasses and no neck.

"Steven, do you have any friends here at school?" he asked, peering at me through those eyes that looked like fish bowls.

"No,"

"Do you have any friends outside of school?"

"I don't know."

"He likes reading books," blurted my mother. "He likes to be by himself."

"Yes," said the Doctor. "Now Steven, do you realize that you are failing the tenth grade?"

"Yes."

"And did you doctor your report cards so your parents

wouldn't find out?"

He held up the report cards that I had fictionalized.

"Yes, I did."

"Do you think that was a good thing for you to do?"

"I guess not."

"Do you know that your parents care about your success here in school?"

"Yes."

"Steven, what can you tell me about this story you wrote, *The Destruction of the Worm*? Do you feel there is a worm inside you?"

"No sir."

"Steven, why do you wear dirty clothes to school? Why don't you brush your hair?"

"I try!" my mother shouted. "What can I do? He won't wash himself. What can I do?"

"Steven, would you mind coming to my office for some informal counseling sessions?"

"No."

"Mr. Jones, do you have any objections?"

My father waited for a second, looking at the doctor through glassy eyes. I heard the engines of his mind warming up.

"We've done all we can," he said finally. "He's impossible."

"Very well then," the doctor finished by saying. "Thank you very much for coming."

My father beat me for faking the report cards but it wasn't a very good beating. His heart wasn't in it. Just a few punches and some swear words and some spitting. But he couldn't keep it up. I was too old now. I had grown bigger than him and I thought I saw something in his eyes which meant he was afraid I might punch back.

"Don't worry, Dad," I said. "I would never hurt you."

"What the hell are you talking about, you little bastard," he yelled, giving me one more punch to the stomach before he stormed out of the room.

After a couple of sessions with the doctor it was agreed that I should be sent away to a special school in Grandville and I was excited. I thought I was about to meet all kinds of people just like me. The last thing I suspected was that I was being sent to an Obedience Camp for Dogs.

MUD AND MINDY

My name is MUD for this part of the story, because after I got in trouble for failing my classes and writing crazy stories I realized that I was Messed Up, and put together with the name "Dad," which is what Kevin called me, you get Messed Up Dad, or MUD for short. Here was me.

And here were all the ordinary people. It was very easy to pick out Messed Up Dad from the line of people.

He was the only one with the stuff growing out of his head—the messed up one. At least that's the way it looked from the outside. If you went inside Messed Up Dad's head you'd find he wasn't messed up—he just didn't belong in this world. But people couldn't see in there, so he got sent away to the special school. They never told him there'd be a bunch of dogs there, Labradors and poodles and German shepherds.

"I'm not a dog!" he said to his mom, and she took him right up to the front row of the class and sat him down next to a Dalmation. Then she left him there in Dog Obedience School and she didn't come back.

Deep inside MUD cried, but on the outside he didn't let anyone know how he felt. He didn't want those dogs thinking he was a baby. He wanted them to think he was better than them, so when the teacher, a fat lady named Mrs. Green, told them to stand up, MUD sat down. And when she told them to sit down, MUD stood up. And when she looked at him with a big smile for the singing lesson, which was *Put on a Happy Face*, when all the dogs smiled and panted and howled, MUD just sat there growling to himself. The only person who knew MUD was crying was a little boy that lived inside MUD's head.

"Don't cry, Dad," said the little boy. "It'll be alright."

In the cafeteria MUD was staring at a plate of dog food when a group of dogs—Chihuahuas and schnauzers, mostly—came over to him and introduced themselves.

"Hi, what's your name," they said.

"MUD," he answered reluctantly. "But I'm not a dog."

"No?" they asked. "What are you?"

"I'm a person," he said.

"We're people, too," they said.

"No you're not," said MUD. "You're just dogs. Get away from me."

"Grrr," the dogs growled and MUD growled back at them and they ran away. MUD went to his cage and lay

there by himself thinking how much better than these stupid dogs he was, because he really was a person and they
were just dogs.

"Yeah," said the little boy in his head. "They're stupid."

And that made MUD feel better. He decided as soon as
he figured out a way, he would run away from the School.

"Yeah," said the little boy. "We'll run away!"

The next morning before classes a girl dog, an Irish setter named Mindy, came up to him and said in a sad little
voice "How are you doing MUD? Are you feeling okay?"

MUD said: "Sure, I'm fine."

That day MUD softened up a little. He still wouldn't do
any of the exercises. And he still thought the dogs were
stupid when they stood up on their hind legs and begged
for food, but he couldn't help noticing this girl dog, Mindy,
with her great red hair and this cute way of wagging her
tail. And his heart jumped when after class she came up to
him again with the sad voice and asked "How are you
doing MUD? Are you okay?"

"Sure," he said bravely. "I'm doing fine."

She kept coming up to him like that every day and MUD
always said he was fine until finally after about a week
when she came up to him and asked him with her gentle,
round eyes, "How are you doing, MUD? Are you feeling
okay?" he burst out crying and told her how miserable he
was feeling, and she listened to him as if she understood
exactly how it was for MUD.

Soon they started hanging around together all the time,
taking walks around the grounds of the school together,
and Mindy talked to MUD about her problems and MUD
felt he understood her just the way she understood him.

She didn't like herself.

She thought she was making a fool of herself all the
time. But she wasn't really making a fool of herself.

Everyone really liked her. But this is what she lived with—a voice in her head telling her that she was stupid and ugly and embarrassing and no good at all.

"I like you, Mindy," MUD said to her, but it didn't seem to make much difference. Her voice still sounded sad. But she was so nice to MUD that MUD decided he wanted to stay in Dog Obedience School, even though he still wouldn't do any of the exercises and even though he growled at Mrs. Green whenever she tried to teach him something. He wanted to stay, though, just so he could be near Mindy, the beautiful Irish setter.

Then one day in the garden in the back of the school Mindy looked up at MUD with a soft look on her face and said "How are you doing MUD? Are you feeling okay?"

And MUD said "Yes, Mindy. Everything's okay when I'm with you."

Then he kissed her on her big wet lips and MUD had never felt anything like it before. All of a sudden

He kissed her with all his heart, with gratitude and love for the way she was with him, and in between kissing he looked in Mindy's eyes and he mumbled, "Mindy, Mindy," and she smiled at him and asked "Does that make you feel better, MUD?"

"Yes," he said.

"Good," she said. "It makes me feel better, too."

They kissed some more and looked at each other some more and all of a sudden something else started growing out of MUD's head, right there in the middle of their kissing.

"Oh no," he said. "Oh no!"

"What is it?" asked Mindy.

"I don't know what it is," MUD lied as the thing grew and grew.

"Don't look," he cried.

"Why not?" asked Mindy.

"I don't want you to see!"

"It's okay, MUD," she said.

So MUD relaxed and it came popping out of his fore-head—the little boy he'd been hiding from the world, a beautiful little boy floating in front of Mindy's face, crying "Mommy! Mommy!"

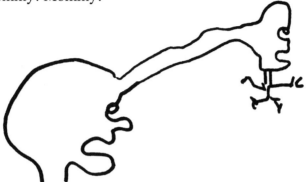

Mindy's face got all dark. She looked down at the ground as though she were ashamed.

"What's the matter!" asked MUD. "You said I didn't have to be ashamed!"

"I know, MUD," she said, and MUD could tell from her voice that she was sorry. "Maybe we shouldn't kiss any more."

"Why not?" asked MUD.

"We just shouldn't," she said. Her tail drooped between her legs and her back was all hunched over, and the little boy was still floating in front of her crying "Mommy."

"Don't you like him?" asked MUD.

"Who?" said Mindy.

"The little boy," he said. "Don't you like the little boy?"

"What little boy?" asked Mindy, though he was right there in front of her face still yelling.

"Don't you see the little boy?" MUD demanded.

"No," she said, shaking her head. "Where is he?"

"Right in front of you," MUD cried. "Don't you see him?"

"No MUD," said Mindy. "I'm sorry."

The little boy popped back in MUD's head as they started walking back to the cages. Mindy wouldn't talk any more. And MUD was confused.

"Why didn't she see you, Kevin?" MUD asked the little boy when he was alone in his cage that night.

"I don't know," said the little boy.

"It must be because I'm a person and she's a dog," said MUD.

"Yeah," said the little boy. "That must be it."

So that night MUD decided that he had to become a dog for Mindy's sake. And from then on he started leading the classes in all the exercises, jumping the highest and running the fastest, and being the first one to get to his cage when Mrs. Green blew her whistle. He won a lot of dog biscuits and did all he could to convince Mindy that he could be as much of a dog as the next guy, but the more MUD did, the sadder Mindy's eyes seemed when she looked at him, and after a while she stopped looking at him altogether, and no longer did she come up to him to ask him how he was feeling. She kept to herself, and MUD knew that his plan wasn't working.

The night before graduation from Dog Obedience School Mrs. Green came to MUD's cage and said "MUD, you really are an inspiration to us all."

"Thank you, Mrs. Green."

"Tomorrow at graduation I'm going to give you the ribbon for best dog!"

"Wow!" said MUD. "Thanks, Mrs. Green."

He ran out of his cage to Mindy's cage and he woke her up shouting "Mindy, Mindy, I won the award for Best Dog!"

"That's great," said Mindy.

But she still looked sad.

"What's wrong, Mindy?" MUD asked. "Please!"

"MUD," she said, "I should have told you a long time ago."

"What?"

Mindy took MUD's hands in her paws and said "MUD, I really think that it's great how well you've been doing in school, and I don't want to hurt your feelings..."

"Hurt my feelings?"

"I already have someone, MUD," she said. "I'm sorry."

"Have someone?"

"A dogfriend."

"You already have a dogfriend?" said MUD, and his feelings *were* hurt. He suddenly felt warm all over as if someone had turned on an electric heater inside him.

"You'll meet him tomorrow when my owners come for the graduation ceremony," she said. "They'll be bringing Max along."

"Max?"

"That's my dogfriend," said Mindy. "He's a Great Dane."

"That's okay, Mindy," MUD said, putting on a brave face. "I'm a person, anyway, and you're a dog. We never could have been together."

"Oh, MUD," cried Mindy, and she tried to hug him, but MUD had gone all cold now, as if the heater had been turned off, and he just wanted to be alone.

"It's okay, Mindy," he said, and went back to his cage.

The next day it happened the way she said—they brought along the big Great Dane.

"MUD!" the Great Dane said in a deep, stupid-sounding voice, shaking his drooling jowls. "I'm pleased to meet you. And thanks for taking care of Mindy here. She says that you've been a real friend!"

MUD looked at Mindy and he couldn't help thinking

that the reason she looked so sad was that she hung around with this big jerk of a dog all the time, and he felt sorry for her. Mindy smiled meekly at MUD as though she felt sorry for him, too, and there wasn't much to say.

MUD went over to meet his parents, who had just driven up into the parking lot in the station wagon.

"Hi, Mom," he said. "Hi, Dad."

"We missed you son!" said his mom. "Why didn't you write us a letter?"

"I was too busy," explained MUD.

"You've lost so much weight," said his mom. "You look so handsome!"

It was true. All the exercises and the dog food had made MUD thinner—he almost looked like a normal person now. But when they called him up to accept the ribbon for Best Dog MUD felt more confused than ever. Everyone else seemed to be happy, but as Mrs. Green placed the ribbon around his neck, MUD looked over at Mindy in the audience as everyone clapped, and felt like running away, it all seemed so stupid.

"Bye, MUD," she said as her owners put her on the leash and led her away.

"Bye, Mindy," said MUD, and that was the end of their love story.

On the way home from Dog Obedience School MUD's father said, "So now you'll be able to make something of yourself, won't you son?"

"Yes, Dad," said MUD.

When he got to his room MUD took the ribbon off and burned it.

"What are we gonna do now?" asked the little boy in his head, and MUD shook his head.

"I don't know, Kev," he said.

MUD looked in at Kevin and remembered how the little

boy had floated right there in front of Mindy's face and she hadn't seen him, and MUD began wondering about the little boy. And for the first time in his life he began thinking of a thing that he didn't let Kevin know about—a secret thing.

THE DESTRUCTION
OF MUD'S WORM

Soon he went back to school. People were nicer to him now that he was thinner. He had started to take better care of his appearance, too, and it seemed that the more he thought about this secret thing, the better he got at fitting in. He even got better at talking to the kids at school. He said things like "Hey Mary, what's up?" and when a guy came up to him and said "Hey MUD, we're having a party this Friday, do you wanna come?" MUD said "You bet!"

At the party he smoked a cigarette and said "Hey, this is a great record!" And afterwards he went out with some guys driving around in a car drinking beers, and MUD shouted "Alright!" The other guys started yelling things out the window of the car, and MUD even shouted something at a girl in a car next to them. "Hey honey!" he shouted, "wanna come for a ride?", and all the guys laughed and slapped MUD on the shoulder. At the end of the night the guys said "Hey, MUD, you're alright!" And they dropped MUD off in front of his house.

When they got up to their room Kevin looked at MUD as if MUD had done something wrong.

"What's the matter, Kev?" asked MUD.

"Nothing," said Kevin. "Let's play with the dolls."

So MUD and Kevin took out the dolls and started imagining things with them, but MUD wasn't concentrating too hard on the dolls. He was concentrating on his secret plan, and Kevin sensed something was wrong.

"Don't you like playing with the dolls no more, Dad?" asked Kevin.

"No," lied MUD. "I'm having fun!"

MUD was holding the doll they had made a long time ago which was the doll called Good Guy, and he knew what Kevin was thinking. Kevin was thinking that MUD had turned into Good Guy.

"Let's go to bed," MUD said.

So they went to bed. Kevin didn't go to sleep, of course. Kevin never slept. He was always right there watching just as MUD would fall asleep, and he'd wait in MUD's head while MUD dreamed, and when MUD woke up in the morning Kevin would always be there, with a bright smile on his face, saying "Mornin', Dad!"

But he never slept himself. He didn't need to because he was a magic child.

Only that night he didn't seem so magical to MUD. He looked more like a worm.

"All this time," thought MUD to himself secretly, "All this time I thought I was different, but now I see there's a worm inside me just as there is inside everyone else. Only it's not in my belly. The worm is in my head."

Then MUD got out of bed.

"Where are we going, Dad?" asked Kevin.

But MUD didn't answer. He put on his clothes, then he sneaked downstairs and went out of the house.

It was the beginning of winter, so there was no snow, but everything seemed hardened and the air was icy on MUD's face as he walked through the town. Nobody was around, and nobody saw him as he headed up the lane to the railroad bridge that cut across the reservoir in the town. The moon was looking down and the cold wind was blowing across the bridge as MUD walked. Then he stopped halfway across the bridge. He heard an owl hooting and a car driving somewhere off in the distance, buzzing like a little fly. MUD looked down. It was such a long way down to the water through the mist. It made his spine tingle just looking at it.

"Dad," peeped the little boy. "Why are we here?"

MUD didn't answer Kevin. Instead, he reached inside his head and plucked out the worm that he thought was growing there inside him, and he threw it off the bridge.

"Dad!" cried Kevin, as he fell down into the fog.

All of a sudden MUD was flying like a bird. But he wasn't really flying at all. He was falling down off the bridge and he was heading toward the water and he could still hear the little worm shouting "Dad!" because the little worm was falling with him.

Then they hit the water and went way down under and MUD saw that the worm wasn't a worm at all. He was a beautiful little boy and he was drowning—his little lungs were filling up with water and he was gurgling.

MUD realized he'd made a terrible mistake.

"Kevin!" he cried, and he tried to save the little boy. He didn't care about himself any more, he just wanted to get the beautiful boy back up to the surface. He swam with all his might but the water was heavy and was pushing him down and everything was black, and soon MUD didn't even know if he was swimming up or down, but just before he passed out MUD felt his head popping above the water.

He didn't know what happened next because he was in a dream and he was crying, holding onto the little boy and hoping he wasn't dead.

"I'm sorry, I'm sorry!" he cried. "Please don't die."

But the little boy was all blue in the face and not moving. MUD just kept holding onto him and praying for life to return.

TEARS

When I woke up in the hospital I was myself again. I knew that what I had inside me was a real, living, breathing thing and it was my very own boy and we didn't belong in Worm Land and my name wasn't MUD.

Standing over me I saw my mother. She was holding my hand.

"Oh Steven," she cried. "Steven, Steven."

"You're alright, boy," I heard someone say, then I saw my father standing on the other side of the bed. "You're alright."

I couldn't talk to them. My whole body seemed to have been broken by the fall. I could only hold my eyes open for the second, then the whole scene disappeared, and I was back in the dream holding onto the little boy.

It went like that for a few days, then I got better and was able to talk. And after a long while I was able to get out of the bed and walk around, so they took me to another hospital, called Grandville Oaks, because they were afraid I might try to kill myself again. In this hospital they watched me all the time, even though I told them my name wasn't MUD any more and that I wasn't going to kill myself ever again. It took a long time but finally I convinced the doctors to send me home.

The first day back was the worst. My mother was crying all during dinner and my dad wasn't saying anything, and the only noise came from the thumping on the window of the snow blowing up against the house.

"Mom, Dad," I said finally, "I'm sorry for what I did."

"We know you are, Steven," said my mother.

"I love you Mom and Dad. I didn't mean you any harm."

"It's not too late," my mom sobbed. "We can make everything better."

Then tears started coming out the side of my dad's eyes too, and that was maybe the worst of it—watching him cry.

"All we care about is you, Son," he said. "We don't care about ourselves. All we want is for you to have a good life. That's all we want."

He put his hand on my wrist and he held it tighter and tighter as though he were trying to convince me by squeezing, as if his words and his crying weren't enough. I felt all his love shooting through me from my wrist and I cried too.

"What should I do, Dad?" I sobbed. "What should I do?"

"Can you go back to school, Son? Can you do that?" he asked, wiping his face with his big hands.

"Yes," I said.

"Let's just start with that, then," he said.

"We'll help you," said my mom. "If you need help you can come to us, you know that."

"Yes, Mom," I said.

"We love you, boy," said my dad, and his whole face was still wet, even though he was pawing at it with his hands. Watching them still crying I vowed that I would stop up the leaky pipes in their eyes. No matter what happened I would never make them cry again—not him or my mom.

"Where are the dolls?" asked Kevin when we got up to my room.

"I don't know," I said. "They must have taken them away."

"It's okay, Dad," said Kev. "We don't have to play with the dolls no more."

"We could make new ones," I said.

"You don't have to, Dad," said Kevin. "And you can go to school and be Good Guy if you want to."

"I won't be Good Guy," I said to Kevin.

"You can do whatever you want," said Kevin. "Don't worry, Dad."

When I went back to school everyone was even nicer to me because they had heard that I'd jumped off the railroad bridge. It was embarrassing how nice they were—even the girls—and I hated every minute of it, but I did it for my father and my mother because I pitied them as much as everyone else pitied me. So I finished high school with grades that were so good that a lot of teachers said I should go to college, but I said, "No, I'm going to be a farmer."

All the other kids left the town, either to go to college or join the army or find work, but I stayed home and helped my father with the work. At night we would all watch television and on Saturdays we'd go for breakfast, not just my dad and me, but my mom now, too, and she loved it. After a few years it was almost as though all the terrible things had never happened.

Then I found the machine.

THE IMPOSSIBLE
  FISH

My dad had kept Lee Roy on at the farm even though I was helping because Lee Roy had a wife and a baby now and no other way of supporting them, so I didn't have much work to do—just a morning's worth.

In the afternoons after I finished my chores I would take my fishing pole and go walking through the town up to Shepherd's Pond, the place I had found that day a long time ago after I was caught with the sheep. Kevin didn't like fishing there at first, because there weren't any fish in the pond, not even a minnow.

"That's why we're fishing here," I told him.

It took him a while to understand why we sat there for hours without a nibble. I wasn't keeping secrets from him—I promised never to do that again—but I was working on a problem that was difficult for him to understand because he was still a little boy. He hadn't grown an inch or gotten any smarter since he first showed up. And he hadn't paid attention in school, so he didn't understand half of what I was thinking about while I sat there in the sun, holding the fishing pole, with the wind jingling the leaves of the trees and smoky white clouds floating in the bright blue sky and little creatures hopping through the green grass. What I was thinking about was a complex theory that I was devising which I hoped would disprove the theory of gravity.

"Dad," Kevin would say when he couldn't stand the boredom any more, "Let's play."

So I would leave off from my calculations and entertain him. We played Impossible Games while our line dangled in the water and the day drifted along, and these games were like the game I was trying to play with gravity, only they were simpler, and a child could play them with enjoyment. There were hundreds of them—the only criterion was that the object of the game be something impossible to do, like holding your breath forever (me and Kev managed to do it for three minutes) or counting to infinity (we got to the trillions before the game got boring). We especially liked the "Think of Nothing" game in which the object was to think of nothing at all.

"Ah ha!" Kevin would cry when he caught me thinking of something, meaning I'd lost the game.

We could go on for hours trying to think of nothing. But our favorite game of all was the Happy Game, where the object was to become impossibly happy.

"I'm so happy," Kev would say, "that I could kiss a cow!"

"And I'm so happy, Kev," I'd respond, "that the moon and stars are my candy treats!"

"I'm so happy that I can speak Chinese!"

"I'm so happy that if I got any happier I'd explode into a million pieces!"

"I'm so happy..."

Through playing these games Kevin eventually came to love going to Shepherd's Pond every day, and he'd leave me alone to work on the problem of gravity as long as I took some time off to play with him.

One day we were sitting there fishing for the Impossible Fish when an airplane appeared in the blue and white sky some 6,000 feet above the pond. I looked up at that air-plane and declared to myself, as I had declared many after-noons before, that there was no reason I shouldn't be able to fly that high myself. And all of a sudden, we weren't fishing any more. We were ascending vertically from the earth.

"Dad!" Kevin cried, "you did it!"

"Yes," I said as I looked down at two boots dangling beneath me like tails of a kite and realized I was already fifty yards up in the air, "I think you're right, Kev."

My body was moving straight up like a vertical lift-off plane, rising up through the air, and soon the pond seemed like a little mud puddle beneath my feet. Finally we got so high up that we could make out the sign written on the tail of the airplane—big blue letters spelling out CESSNA.

"Wow!" cried Kevin with delight as we rose to the same level as the plane and it went soaring past us. We were even able to discern the perplexed face of the middle-aged pilot in the cockpit of the plane. His whole head shook as though he was seeing a UFO when he spotted us there, floating in the sky like Mary Poppins, holding our fishing rod out to the air like fishermen of the clouds.

"Hi!" Kevin yelled as the airplane went past.

Then my powers of levitation began to fail and we began heading back down towards the little mud puddle, as though there was an invisible parachute guiding our descent, and soon we were sitting there fishing again at the pond as though nothing had happened.

"Do it again! Do it again!" cried Kev.

But I didn't want to do it again. I had proved my point—gravity was a word invented by the worm-people to keep the world boring, and I didn't have to put up with it. I was the Impossible Dad and my powers had not deserted me, even though I was far from home and so much time had

passed since I'd left that magical place. With a great deal
of work I could remember them.

"Please, Dad," cried Kev because he had loved our little
test flight so much, but I had already moved onto my next
experiment, which was disproving the worm theory of
time.

"Dad! Come on!"

"No, Kev," I said, looking at the sun, which was high up
in the sky but soon would be setting. And the secret of time
seemed even more elusive than the secret of gravity.

"Time," I thought to myself that day as we trekked
home. "Where is it?"

I looked at my watch on my wrist. The second hand was
spinning slowly around a circle of numbers.

"But where is time?" I wondered. "This watch proves
nothing."

A while later, after I'd been thinking about my theory of
time for a couple of weeks, my dad drove us into
Grandville after our Saturday breakfast and we visited the
County Zoo. Kevin was so wild about the monkeys that we
stayed in the monkey house for hours watching them while
my parents walked around by themselves. It was a warm
spring day and my parents looked as if they were having a
good time, too. They were holding hands and feeding the
animals, and the whole thing was about the nicest day we'd
ever had as a family. When my parents came back into the
monkey house to tell us it was time to go I had an idea. I
took out a little piece of paper from a notebook and scribbled down some calculations in the form of a sentence.

"A message to the future," I wrote. *"When you read this
you will remember having written it."*

I tore out the piece of paper and crumpled it up in the
pocket of my overalls. Then I caught up with my parents

and we drove home.

Time passed.

It was a month later. It was raining and me and Kev were fishing again at Shepherd's pond. Kev started getting whiny because the rain was falling and we were getting wet and cold. It was then I had my breakthrough.

I took out the crumpled piece of paper from my pocket and I read back what I had written all those weeks ago in the Monkey House. *"A message to the future. When you read this you will remember having written it."*

I did remember, too. I remembered very well. It was like drilling a hole in the wall of time and seeing that day when we were in Grandville watching the monkeys.

"Come on, Kev," I said and Kev followed me through the hole, and we were back there jumping up and down and laughing at the monkeys. All by looking into a crumpled up piece of paper! But just like the flying experiment, it only worked for a while. Soon the power wore off and we stopped remembering, and found ourselves back at Shepherd's Pond—fishing in the rain.

"Come on, Kev," I said. "Let's go home."

"But I wanna see the monkeys!" he complained.

I knew it wouldn't work any more. I crumpled up the paper and threw it into the pond—and suddenly I had the strangest feeling. My face went all cold and my head got dizzy as I watched the little piece of paper falling toward the water.

"What's the matter, Dad?" asked Kev.

"Nothing," I muttered. "I'm alright."

But the feeling lasted a long time, all the way home through the rain. I was sure that I had done it before! A long time ago I had thrown something into that very same pond—I knew it. It was like a feeling they call *déjà vu.* And even though I had forgotten it soon enough, I mention it here because later on something happened which proved it was a real memory.

Before I go on to that, though, I have to tell about my next experiment and the space suit.

THE SPACE SUIT

I found it up in the attic one day in an old chest full of things which belonged to my grandfather.

"What is it?" asked Kev.

"It's the space suit we wore when we came from the Impossible Land," I told him.

There was a black tail coat and a thick cotton shirt that smelled like the past, all soaked with some sort of cologne my grandfather must have worn. There was a black bow tie, too, and an old sweet smelling corn cob pipe, which had little nibbles on the end of it which must have come from my grandfather's teeth. Then there was our favorite thing—two cuff links in the shape of stars that kept the shirt sleeves together.

"These are the tiny stars from outer space," I told Kevin. "We plucked them on our journey here and kept 'em as souvenirs."

"But Dad," asked Kevin. "These are Grandpa's clothes, aren't they?"

"No," I said. "We just disguised them as Grandpa's clothes. When we get into outer space they turn into a radiation-proof space suit."

"Steven!" my mother said when I came downstairs. "What are you doing in those old clothes?"

"Nothing, Mom."

"But they don't even fit you, Son," she said.

I looked down at my thighs, squeezed tightly into the black trousers and my belly bursting out of the tightly buttoned tail coat and I had to agree—but I liked the clothes too much to let that stop me.

"They're alright, Mom," I told my mom as I grabbed my fishing gear. When I bent down to tie my shoes I felt a little rip between my legs.

"Dad," Kev said. "You broke the space suit!"

"I know, Kev," I said. "We'll need that hole for ventilation in outer space."

Walking through the town in the suit that day I thought: if my grandfather could see the town now with its carpet outlets, its video store, its new highway—he wouldn't recognize it. In the twenty years since I had been alive it had gone from being a small cow town to a place where rich people lived, commuting to Grandville for work.

I stopped at the Seven Eleven, as I always did on my way to fishing, to get my Mountain Dew and Ding Dongs. Everyone in the store looked at me as though I were a ghost from the past.

"Dad," said Kev. "Everyone's looking at you."

But I was well practiced in the art of "fitting in" with the people in my town.

"Don't worry, Kev," I said.

Grabbing my Ding Dongs I proceeded to the counter and, looking away from the counterman's face as I spoke, I said the most ordinary, unimaginative thing I could think of.

"Not too busy today, are ya?" I said.

"Nope," said the man, looking away from my eye. "Not too busy at all."

Suddenly everyone in the store stopped staring at me

and turned their eyes to the floor.

"Nice goin', Dad," said Kev.

The citizens of my town, I should mention, had a secret agreement which was: when meeting, to say only the most obvious thing, and to look away from one another's eyes when uttering the agreed upon saying. "Mornin', Jim," Joe had to say when meeting Jim. "How goes it?"

"Oh, not too bad," Jim had to mutter in reply, avoiding the speaker's gaze and choosing an object—a wall calendar, maybe, or a countertop—to focus his attention on. "And how goes it with you?"

"Slow and steady," Joe had to reply. "Slow and steady."

And both had to laugh for no reason at all, before nodding and bidding farewell with "I'll see ya when I see ya."

From going around to pick up feed and equipment with my father I had gotten very good at looking away from people's faces and saying unimaginative things. Even though everyone had heard about me jumping off the bridge, by now I had begun to overhear people saying things to my father like "He's a real chip off the old block, ain't he?", which in the code of the town's language was a safe way of saying that they were glad I had gotten better and that they were happy for my father and that they loved my father, they loved him so much, he was one of the tribe and they understood his suffering and their hearts went out to him. They couldn't come out and say it like that—there was, after all, the agreement—but that's what they meant.

"Have a nice day," said the man behind the counter, handing me my bag of Mountain Dew and Ding Dongs.

"You too," I said, and I marched triumphantly out of the store in my Grandfather's clothes as though they were the most ordinary things to be wearing on this fine spring morning.

THE MARAUDERS

Outside the Seven Eleven I encountered a group of indi-
viduals who didn't keep to the "agreement," and made
some abusive comments about my appearance.

"Preacher," they yelled. "Here comes the Preacher."

They were the gang of kids who hung around in front of
the Seven Eleven playing loud music on big radios and
generally snarling at you as you went into the store. The
young men wore leather jackets and tattoos, the women
wore short skirts and lace stockings and had frizzy hair and
lots of makeup on. They were always there in front of the
store looking like a gang of outlaws, but they had never
bothered me before, and it came as a surprise that of all the
people in the town, these "non-conformists" would be the
ones to voice objection to my unorthodox costume.

"Hey, Preacher," one of them said, grabbing my bag of
treats, "what you got in the bag?"

I didn't fight back. I let them steal my Ding Dongs and
push me around. But when they grabbed my fishing pole
Kevin encouraged me to take some sort of defensive
action.

"Dad," he said, "don't let 'em do that."

"Gentlemen, ladies," I began.

"Ah ha ha ha!" they laughed.

"I mean you no harm," I said. "Please, return my fishing
pole."

"Sure, Preacher," one of them said, a big guy with a beard and crooked teeth. "Here you go, Preacher."

He busted the fishing pole in two and handed the pieces back to me.

"Why did you do that?" I asked the man, whose face was glaring so close to my own that I smelled the sour odor of beer wafting outward between the crooked spikes that were his teeth.

"Aw," he mocked me. "I'm sorry, Preacher."

The others roared with laughter.

I turned away and headed for the road. My back was pelted with Ding Dongs and empty Mountain Dew cans.

"Dad!" said Kev.

"Forget it," I said. "They don't mean any harm."

I tried to put the incident out of my mind. But the next day after my chores I wondered if it was such a good idea to wear the space suit after all.

"Come on, Dad," encouraged Kev. "Don't be afraid."

I squeezed into the pants and headed out. My first stop was the Western Auto, where I purchased a new fishing rod. Even though there were no fish in the pond, fishing with the broken stick that had been left me by the "marauders" (as I had dubbed the gang of kids) had felt foolish. With my new pole in hand I proceeded to the Seven Eleven.

"Preacher," the marauders cried as I walked past. I ignored them. I came out of the store with more Mountain Dew and Ding Dongs than usual.

"Gentlemen, ladies," I said, passing out cans to each of them. "These are for you. A peace offering. Do you accept?"

"Oh, Preacher," the big bearded one said. "We're sorry."

"Apology accepted," I said.

"Is that a new pole you got there?" he asked, grabbing

my pole.

"Yes," I said. "Please don't break it."

"Ah ha ha ha," they laughed, but not as heartily as before.

"We won't break it," said the bearded one. "Go on, Preacher, good fishing to you."

He handed me back the rod.

We had achieved a settlement. After that, the marauders took an avid interest in my fishing career.

"Catch anything, Preacher?" they would ask.

"No, no," I would say.

But I wasn't exactly speaking the truth. Even though my hook continued to emerge from that water without the slightest nibble, my latest experiment was proceeding at a breathtaking pace.

FISHING ON THE GRANDVILLE EXPRESS

I knew from my reading that in the past philosophers had given various locations to the soul. Some had thought of the heart as the place people "live." Some had even thought of the liver or the spleen. Eastern philosophers had given special importance to a place just below the navel as the seat of the energy that is the soul. But nowadays it seems to have become accepted that inside everybody's head is a little person that is the soul or the self, even though everybody knows if you cut open a skull you won't find it. Supposedly that's because the soul is invisible.

In my head of course there was a little boy named Kevin and there was no doubt that he lived in my head. And somewhere, invisibly surrounding him was me—Dad.

But once I had seen Kevin pop out of my head and float in the air in front of another—the girl-dog Mindy.

The hypothesis of my experiment was that I too could pop out of my head and be somewhere far away from my head or the body that was fishing next to the pond, dressed in the space suit. My hypothesis was that I could return to the Impossible Land, while leaving my body here. My hypothesis was that I could be in two places at the same time.

In my previous work I had overcome the limits of gravity and time, but I had taken my body with me when I flew up into the sky, or when I stepped through the wall of the present into the past. This was impressive, yes, but it served no purpose. Even if I developed my theoretical "powers" to a point where return to the Impossible Land was within my reach, there would always be the problem of my parents. They needed me—my body, my presence. My absence would hurt them. Thus my experiment: I would divide myself into two mutually exclusive parts— my body and my soul. Then, perhaps, I could escape.

I had to start with the basics. My first attempt while fishing was to place my consciousness not within the fisherman, but a few feet down the bank to the left. From there I attempted to observe the man dressed in the tail coat/space suit, smoking the corn cob pipe and dangling the line in the water. I attempted to be "elsewhere" from my body. My method could be formulated thus: think of a number, any number—now imagine that you are that number.

I thought of the number 63, but I didn't think it in my head. I thought it five yards down the bank. Then I thought of the number 5,654, but again, I didn't think it as a symbol in my consciousness. I thought of it as myself, floating freely above some reeds in the shallow green water, 10 yards from my body. Then I thought of the number 456, but I didn't think of it as three digits inside a thought. I became the beautiful monument "456" which was floating in the middle of the pond like a fountainhead. Finally I imagined I was a very daring number—354,908—standing proudly miles to the north, towards Grandville, on top of the mountain called Grey Lock.

I was exhausted. Standing on top of this mountain I could see our little town, nestled in a valley like a little diorama, as though the houses were made of *papier-maché*. I couldn't see the Shepherd's Pond—it was hidden by a cluster of trees that looked like twigs. But I could imagine my body there, holding the fishing pole.

"Dad," I heard someone call.

Kevin missed me.

"Here I am, Kev," I said, coming back into my head.

"Where did you go, Dad?"

"Nowhere, Kev," I said.

But over the weeks I continued with my experiments, traveling as far as the next county simply by imagining numbers. Gradually Kevin began to get the idea and began imagining numbers with me, and together we would journey elsewhere from our body.

"What's it doing without us?" Kevin asked me one day while we imagined the number 3,098,235 sitting on the Grandville Express train, chugging thirty miles north of the city.

"It's fishing," I told him. "Keep imagining."

Three million ninety-eight thousand two hundred thirty-five," Kev said.

"Thataboy Kev," I said. "Soon we'll be able to imagine our way back to the Impossible Land and everything will be wonderful!"

"Dad!" Kevin cried out.

"What's the matter?"

"Dad!" he cried again. "Something's wrong!"

Suddenly we weren't on the train any more. We were flying through space back to Shepherd's Pond, and when we got there we found the body, dressed in my grandfather's suit, slumped over on the bank, the fishing rod floating in the shallow water. When I got back inside I felt a sickness I'd never felt before—everything was swirling around like a whirlpool. The body was gagging and coughing.

"Stop imagining!" I yelled at Kevin.

"I'm not imagining!" he yelled back.

"We're dying" I said to Kevin.

"No, Dad!" he said.

Suddenly the body puked up a pile of Ding Dong/Mountain Dew soup on the side of the river and the wave of sickness passed. I sat up and looked out through bleary eyes at the water.

"We're okay, Kev," I said. "We're okay."

"Dad," he said, his voice all hoarse and weak. "Let's not play that game any more."

"Come on, Kev," I said. "Let's go home."

CLARA

Spring was nearing its end. It rained almost every afternoon and many afternoons I didn't bother going fishing. Instead I stayed in my room typing a story on the typewriter that my mother had bought me for Christmas.

"Thanks, Mom," I had told her halfheartedly because then I was still a scientist and writing stories seemed baby stuff.

Since my last experiment I wasn't sure about my science any more. It was clear now that no matter what brilliant theory I invented, I was still and always would be trapped in a double bind—I could not live here in the Land of Worms, and yet I had to live here in the Land of Worms. I was a prisoner whose escape would mean his death, and no science could save me from that destiny.

Desolate as I had become it was my only solace to try to create an exact diagram on that typewriter to represent my sorry condition. Not that it would help, my condition would remain sorry. But there was nothing else for me to do.

One day in late May, though, the sun was peeking out of the clouds shyly, and a flock of swallows returning from the south were chirping so merrily that when Kevin said "Come on, Dad, let's go fishing" I could hardly refuse. I put on the space suit, grabbed the fishing pole and headed for the Seven Eleven.

"Preacher!" cried the marauders. "Where you been?"

I headed past them without reply and emerged from the store with my fishing snacks. Suddenly I felt a claw clamp down on my shoulder.

"Unhand me," I snapped.

"Preacher," said the big bearded guy who had been my previous tormentor, "come with us, we want a word with you."

He lifted me up and carried me around to the back of the store, followed by his giggling sidekick.

"Take my Ding Dongs!" I cried. "Put me down!"

"Take it easy, Preacher," he said. "We ain't gonna hurt you."

He put me down. Then I saw her, in back of the cinder block wall of the Seven Eleven, with her shirt half off. She was sitting in a pile of weeds as though in a trance.

"Clara," the bearded guy said, "you know the Preacher..."

"The Preacher's next! The Preacher's next!" giggled the sidekick.

But the girl just sat there with her legs folded up beneath her, staring at the gravel and the weeds.

"Clara!" coaxed the bearded guy. "Don't you like the Preacher?"

Then the girl looked up at me. She had dyed blonde hair and a little purse hanging from her arm, embroidered with a fire-breathing dragon. Her stockings were torn. Those were the only three things I remember about her—her hair, her purse and her stockings. And one other thing: the way she looked at me. She looked up at me as if I were invisible and she couldn't see me at all. I didn't like it.

"Gentlemen," I said, "excuse me."

I tried to go but they grabbed me.

"Not so fast, Preacher."

Then the girl spoke.

"Leave him alone, Kurt," she said.

Her voice was a powerful thing, like a voice that knows everything there is to know and commands the listener. As soon as she spoke I felt the claws releasing my shoulders.

"Just leave him be," she said again, and it surprised me that sitting there on the stones looking bleary-eyed with her shirt pulled off her shoulder she could talk like that, with that authority, but right away the tough guys started sounding like naughty children.

"We were only kidding," they said. "You're not mad, are you Clara?"

I looked at the girl and she looked right through me again toward something else.

"Go on, Preacher," the bearded guy said, "get out of here."

THE MACHINE

Ididn't feel like going fishing after that unpleasant encounter, but Kevin insisted. We hiked up to Shepherd's Pond as usual, but the joy of fishing was gone. I had no experiments to work on.

"Let's play a game," said Kev.

"I don't feel like it," I said.

So we sat there doing nothing with the line dangling in the water and I couldn't stop thinking about the girl and the three things about her and the other thing—the way she looked at me. Finally the sun started going down behind the trees and I was glad. I stood up and started reeling in the line.

"Dad!" cried Kevin suddenly. "You got one!"

"Impossible," I said, because I knew there weren't any fish in Shepherd's Pond. But for some reason my line wouldn't reel in and the pole was bending down toward the water. The Impossible Fish had been hooked!

"Pull it in, Dad. Pull it in!"

"Alright," I yelled.

The fish was tugging so hard at the line that soon I was being dragged two feet into the water.

"Damn it!" I said, regaining my balance and thinking about my Grandfather's trousers all splattered now with mud.

"Go Dad, go!"

I got myself out of the water but the fish was pulling even harder now.

"What should I do, Kev?" I shouted.

"Pull it in!"

The weight seemed to get heavier the more I reeled in. I dug my heels into the mud. Kevin shouted and cheered me on but I was beginning to feel uneasy about the whole project.

"What is it?" cried Kev. "Is it a trout?"

"I don't know," I said, trying to get a glimpse of it in the water, but all I saw was a deep dark green. I began envisioning some sort of monster lurking there under the water, a terrible beast which had been disturbed from some primeval slumber and was about to leap out of the water and eat both of us.

"Maybe we should let it be," I said to Kev.

Then the fear spoke even louder in my voice.

"Maybe we should run away!"

"Run away?" exclaimed Kev, and he looked at me as if I had just proven something about my character that he had suspected all along: I was a coward.

"It might be dangerous," I tried to explain.

Kevin frowned at me.

I stood my ground, if only to appear brave before the boy. I pulled in my line. Bubbles were rising to the surface. The weight grew more mighty. Finally a dark presence could be detected below the surface where my line entered the water, a dark seething mammoth presence there which I brought in like a hero. And although Kevin was disappointed, I was greatly relieved when, landed on the bank, the thing proved itself to be—in fact—an inanimate object.

"It's not a fish," cried Kevin.

We went over to the bank where a harmless-looking

black blob of a thing was sitting lifelessly, covered in sick-ly green slime.

"No, it's not a fish," I agreed, cutting the line away from the mass. "We must have snagged it off the bottom."

But as we stood there above the black and green lump I noticed a kind of glow emanating from its metal shell, a kind of hopeful way of looking at me that it had—a friend-liness about it that warranted closer inspection. I kicked it with my boot just to make sure that it was dead.

"Come on, Kev," I said. "Let's take it home."

We wrapped it in my grandfather's tail coat and headed down the path toward town. It was heavy and dripping and I had to put it down to rest several times before reaching home. When I tried to sneak past my mother in the kitchen on the way up to my room I was defeated by the puddle of green and black ooze in our wake.

"Steven Jones!" she called up the stairs. "Come back here this instant."

I left the machine on the landing and went back down.

"I'm sorry, Mom," I said. "I fell in the pond. I'll clean it up."

"What was that you were carrying?" She frowned at me.

"Nothing, Mom," I answered. I got some paper towels and started wiping the scum from the floor. My mom glanced toward the stairs suspiciously, but then she went back to the dishes.

When the floor was clean I ran up and took the machine into the bathroom where we washed off all the ooze in the tub. My mother knocked on the door after we had been in there about an hour.

"Steven! What are you doing in there?"

"Be out in a minute, Mom."

We cleaned up real good, using a toothbrush for the hard-to-reach parts, and when we were sure that the coast was clear, wrapped the machine in a towel and ran into my bedroom and put it on the floor.

"What is it, Dad?" asked Kev.

"I don't know," I said, looking at the strange black box. "It's real old, isn't it?"

"Yeah," said Kev. "But what is it?"

Now that it was clean, little black buttons with letters on them could be seen on the front of the machine. And underneath its front cover there were little metal hammers and spools and gears and cogs.

I looked up at my desk where the electric typewriter my mother had bought me for Christmas was perched. I looked back at the machine on my floor.

"Well," I said at last. "It's just a real old typewriter, isn't it?"

"Da-ad," he frowned.

He didn't believe me.

"Sure it is!" I claimed. "Look!"

I hit one of the buttons with my finger. The keys didn't respond.

"If it's a typewriter, why ain't it typing?" asked Kevin suspiciously.

"It's gotten rusted from being under water so long."

He still didn't believe me.

"Da-ad," he reminded me. "No secrets, right?"

"No secrets," I agreed, and I couldn't keep it up any more. "You're right," I confessed. "It's not a typewriter."

Kev started jumping up and down, his little eyes popping out of their tiny sockets.

"Dad, is it true?"

I remembered the uncanny *déjà vu* feeling from months ago when I had thrown a piece of crumpled paper into the water. But this wasn't *déjà vu* any more. This was something clear in my memory: years and years ago Kevin and I had thrown this very machine into the water in Shepherd's Pond. Then I had turned to him and said "Come on, Kev, let's go," and we had floated across the town to the farm-house where a woman was delivering her first and only child. And we had been born inside Steven Jones.

"Yes, Kev," I admitted, "we have found the Machine."

DELAYS

The next day it was sunny again but we didn't go fishing. Instead we got some tools from the barn and began working on the machine with my bedroom door locked. We screwed and unscrewed. We took it all apart and we oiled all the inner workings of the machine's intestines.

"How does it work, Dad?" asked Kev.

I remembered it all now. I explained to Kevin that when we were in the Impossible Land we had been able to type just one word into the machine to start it up.

"What word?"

"Well," I said, "the word was on."

"Start it up, Dad!" Kev cried.

I inserted a piece of paper into the machine. Putting my fingers to the black buttons I type the word on.

The keys hit the paper but no writing came out. And the machine didn't turn on.

"Da-ad," sighed Kev.

"The ribbon has gotten ruined," I said.

"Can we get a new ribbon?" he cried. "Can we?"

"Sure," I said.

"And what do we do after we get it turned on, Dad?"

I told him that after we got it started the machine would

do whatever we wanted it to do. If we wanted it to fly, all we had to do was type the word fly, and if we wanted it to fly faster, all we'd have to do was type the word faster, and if we wanted to turn left, all we had to do was type turn left, and so forth.

"We gotta get a new ribbon, Dad!" cried Kev.

I felt bad. Kevin was so happy about finding the machine, but I knew we could never really use it because of my "double bind." I had to be an ordinary person. I had to stay with my parents and we could never fly away on a machine, no matter how wonderful.

"It won't make any difference," I told him.

"Why not?"

"Because," I told him, "before I threw it in the water I programmed the machine with a secret code so that it could never be used, even if someone found it."

"What's the secret code?"

"Well," I said, "the code is so secret that even I can't remember it until it's the right time."

"Maybe it's the right time now, Dad!"

"I don't think so," I said.

"But let's at least get the ribbon and give it a try," he said.

"Okay," I said. "We'll get the ribbon."

The next afternoon I put the machine in a duffel bag and took it to the stationery store on Main Street. The man behind the counter was puzzled.

"Got no brand name," he said, looking all around the machine. "Never seen a typewriter like it."

"Well," I said, "I guess if it's got no brand name, we can't buy a ribbon for it."

I felt a moment of relief, but then the man said: "Well, I can order a ribbon custom-made if you want. That's what they do for old machines like this one. It'll cost you, though."

"Yay!" cried Kevin.

The man took measurements of the machine and told me it would take about four weeks. I paid him and took the machine back home, where I hid it under my bed.

Kevin wanted to look at it all the time, asking questions about how it worked. I eventually told him that the more questions you asked the less chance you'd have of getting the machine to work.

"You just gotta have faith," I said.

"Do you have faith, Dad?" asked Kev.

"Sure I do," I said.

We didn't have anything to do in the afternoons. Fishing didn't make sense. I kept on typing my story on the Christmas typewriter, but I couldn't concentrate. I kept worrying about what I would do when the ribbon came and how I would be able to convince Kevin that we couldn't leave. To calm down I spent a lot of afternoons just walking around the town trying to think of nothing at all.

"It's alright, Dad," Kevin said one day while I was staring in through the furniture store on Main Street. "We don't have to go back to the Impossible Land. But we can fly around on the machine and have fun when the ribbon comes. Can't we?"

"Sure," I said. "But don't forget about the secret code."

"Oh, yeah," he said. "The secret code."

"I'm sorry, Kev," I said.

"Dad," he said then, less disappointed sounding than I'd expected. "I'm hungry. Let's go buy a Ding Dong."

"Okay, Kev," I said.

I walked down the street toward the little candy store.

"No, Dad," he said. "Let's not get the Ding Dong there."

"Why not?"

"Let's go to Seven Eleven, Dad," he said.

"I don't wanna do that, Kev," I said.

I hadn't been to the Seven Eleven since the guys had hassled me last.

"They won't bug us, Dad," said Kev. "You don't even have the space suit on!"

My Grandpa's suit reminded me of the space machine and the double bind, and lately I had been walking around the town in my overalls. But even though I was dressed normally I didn't want to go to the Seven Eleven for another reason, and that reason was the girl who had looked at me so strangely.

I headed into the Super Duper.

"No, Dad," said Kev. "Not the Super Duper! The Seven Eleven!"

"Alright," I said.

KEVIN'S MOM

I was in the parking lot heading toward the kids hanging around in front, hoping they wouldn't recognize me in my overalls.

"Preacher!" they shouted. "Out of uniform?"

I was staring straight ahead, moving like a battering ram, thinking I would barge through the line of kids, when something caught my eye and I lost all my confidence. It was her.

She looked better—not drunk—and she was wearing just jeans and a T-shirt with a picture of some fire and brimstone scene which I knew had something to do with the music the marauders listened to, which was blaring out of their huge radio.

She looked at me—she looked through me, rather. Then I noticed Kevin getting redder than I'd ever seen him.

"Preacher," someone teased as she stared at me and I stared at her, "I think it's love."

Kevin was making a funny face at the girl as though he were embarrassed. He curled his mouth up in folds, then he stuck his tongue out at her, and at the exact moment he did so, I saw something on the face of the girl—a response, like a twitching of the lips outward, the tiniest little smile, as though she were smiling at Kevin.

"Ah ha ha!" laughed the marauders. "Ayyyy," screamed the music on their radio. And then "Ah ha ha ha," the guys were laughing again, and she was looking through me with burning eyes —the most painful-looking eyes, as though behind each one there was a tiny red devil poking at the back of her eyeballs with a hot poker.

I remembered the doll I had made years ago to represent Mara and the little rubies I'd pasted onto her eyes.

"No," I said out loud.

Then they laughed louder. I couldn't look at the burning eyes any more. Suddenly I was pushing past the girl into the Seven Eleven.

"She sees you!" I was saying to Kevin.

"It's okay, Dad," he said, but he was still all bashful-looking and I was scared.

"How do you know it's okay?" Seething, I stared at a shelf full of potato chips, forgetting what I had come in for.

"She won't hurt us," he said.

"She might," I said. "She's a strange girl."

"It's okay," he said.

Kevin wasn't looking at me any more. He had started looking away, and when I followed the direction of his eyes, I saw her outside the window of the store, staring in—watching us.

I grabbed some Ding Dongs and went to the counter.

"Who is that?" I said to the man behind the cash register.

"Beg your pardon?"

I realized I was doing two things wrong. First—I was looking straight at the man's face as I spoke to him instead of looking down at the counter the way people are supposed to in my town. Second, I was saying something to him slightly out of the ordinary.

"I'm sorry," I said, glancing away. "That sure is a weird girl looking in through that window."

"Oh," he said, noticing the girl. "Yeah, she's weird alright. Her name's Clara Price. I think she comes from the Bee Hive."

"The Bee Hive," I said. "Thank you."

I left the Ding Dongs on the counter. I didn't look at Clara Price as we went out the door. I didn't listen to them laughing and I didn't pay any attention to the can of beer that hit me hard on the back of the neck as I made my escape until I was almost home. Then I felt a stinging behind my head. When I got into my room I was shivering. It wasn't because of the blood trickling down my neck that I shivered. It was because I was remembering.

It was just like the day I had remembered throwing something into the pond as a *déjà vu*. I could feel it clinging to the furthest extreme of my memory. I knew I had seen that girl somewhere before. It wasn't even in this lifetime and it wasn't even on this planet. And her name wasn't Clara when I had seen her last. When I had seen her last her name was Mara and she was the Mother of the Impossible Child. She was me. I was her. We both were Kevin. Everything had been connected—

"It's okay," Dad," said Kevin, but I was shivering on my bed sheets, which were dotted with little drops of blood from my cut.

"N-n-no," I stuttered, shivering. "N-n-no, K-k-ev-v-vin, it-t's n-not ok-k-kay at-t all."

THE VIRUS

I knew who Clara Price was. Her father had been a drink-ing partner of my own father, long ago. But Clara Price's father didn't go to the hospital like my dad. Instead he had run away with a barmaid and deserted his family. I had gone to school with Clara Price's older brother, Danny, who helped support the family by working in a gas station fixing cars after school. But one night during our senior year he had gotten himself killed on his motorcycle, and since the family had nothing to live on after that, they ended up moving into the Bee Hive.

There is a small slum in my town, just one block long, and on this block is a huge broken down house called the Bee Hive, because it seems to the passerby that there are thirteen families living there, swarming around like so many insects. Dirty children hang out of all the windows and fat women sit on the front porch smoking brown ciga-rettes, in polyester clothes, frowning at you as you walk past. And when you pass you smell something thick in the air coming from the depths of the hive, like dirty fingers reaching out, trying to drag you inside the swamp of squalor and empty bottles and garbage that you imagine lurks inside, so you stop taking the direct route to town— through the slum—because you don't want to know any

106

more than you already do.

People made up stories: that there were ghosts and dead bodies and murderers living inside there, and prostitutes. Young boys told each other things they had seen or imagined through the upper yellow windows, women in bras doing things you only read about in magazines. But I was never sure if they were true, these stories, or just things made-up to make the horrible place seem more exotic. I never paid much attention.

From these depths emerged this girl, Clara Price, who didn't have red hair like Mara, the doll I had made in my childhood. Instead she had blonde hair, a white, unreal blonde, and she hung around in the streets with the other children of that slum, smoking cigarettes with snarls on their pale, weary faces. If they didn't die the way Clara's brother had the men would end up in prisons and the women would end up pregnant, sitting on the porch with their fat mothers, scowling at the passersby. Or maybe they would disappear like Clara's father to another county, never to be heard from again. Clara was at the early arc of this cycle. She couldn't have been more than eighteen, and yet she already wore the scorn of a hundred years of suffering. I couldn't guess what caused her to scorn like that, through eyes that sizzled like frying eggs. I didn't want to know.

I didn't want to know anything about her because I knew too much already. I knew she wasn't really Clara Price, and I knew that I had loved her the way I loved Kevin—she wasn't separate from me. We had been perfectly together and inextricable from one another, like the front and back of a hand. We had been delightful to one another once. Everything we said to one another we had spoken out of kindness and appreciation of the other. Our love had been the kind of love that is impossible here where everything separates and decays. But then she had eaten the worm...

I didn't want to remember.

"How are we gonna get the worm out of her, Dad?" asked Kevin.

"I don't know," I said. "I don't know."

But Kevin knew that I knew. There was a potion somewhere here in the Land of Worms that would dissolve the worm and then we could go back... But I didn't want to think about it.

I didn't want to go out, either. After we saw her that second time and came home shivering I couldn't go anywhere. It took all my energy to hold the shivering back during breakfast with my parents, and all my might to keep it from my dad in the fields—this thing that was possessing me like a disease and making me shiver. When we were finished with lunch, telling them I was going upstairs to work on a story I rushed to my room and then I finally gave in to the disease and fell shaking on my bed like a man with malaria.

Kevin tried to calm me down.

"Don't worry, Dad. Don't worry."

But nothing he said made any difference. I had the disease that comes from being in an Impossible Situation. One of me had to go to her, had to give her the potion and fly away on the machine never to return. Another of me had to forget her and stay with my parents and be good and ordinary and not crazy.

"We don't have to go back," said Kevin as I shivered. "It's okay, Dad. I don't mind."

"Yes," I thought. "We can be happy here, the three of us! We don't have to go back. We can be together here!"

But Kevin looked at me now in a funny way, and I started shivering again. I knew that this was the most impossible thing of all—for Clara Price to like me. To Clara Price and the marauders I was a fool. Not a man at all. An idiot who wore a ridiculous black costume and walked around town like a lonely stupid turd that no one wanted to be with, least of all someone like Clara Price. It was the other in her that liked me, loved me, adored me, *was* me... I was shaking at the impossibility of it all. It was Mara, whose hair was red, not blonde, who loved me, hidden inside Clara the way I was hidden inside Steven Jones. It was the presence of Mara that made me shiver on my bed.

"It's not okay," I would say to Kevin.

Now everything was an emergency. From day to night there was a virus in my life. It took all my concentration to make the virus so small it wouldn't be seen as I sat there watching television with my parents at night. Once my hand started shaking, the virus had gotten in there and was spinning around and around. I tried to make the virus small but it was too late. My mother had caught the twitching with her eye.

"Son?" she asked. "Are you alright?"

In her face I noticed there weren't nearly so many shadows as there had once been, and I knew why. It was because of that secret agreement I had made with my parents on my first day back from the hospital, the agreement which I had signed with my own blood—that I would pretend forever, or at least until they died, that nothing was wrong with me and everything was ordinary, casual, okay. I saw how bright that agreement had made her face. Now she depended on my pretending. I couldn't go back on it.

In my father's face I saw how calm he had become, how still he was sitting on the leather reclining chair, with undisturbed eyes, because he had a "chip off the old block." He could never know I was succumbing to an Impossible Disease. It would ruin all those years of work... all that rigorous pretending.

"Of course, Mom," I said, "everything's fine."

II
VISITS

FIRST CALLERS

One afternoon as I lay shaking on my bed I heard a car pulling into the driveway. In a few moments my mother was knocking at my door. I made the virus that made me shiver tiny, tiny, tiny so that there was just an invisible convulsing in my stomach when my mother entered the room. She was smiling, happier than I'd ever seen her, as though her whole face had been lit with a magic candle.

"Steven," she said, "there's a girl here to see you."

"Tell her to go away!" I shouted.

The virus transferred to my shoulders, which started seizing up and down.

"Steven!" she said.

She was so happy that she wasn't even there in the room with me. She was off in a dream that had arrived at the door and carried her away like a tornado—she was dreaming that finally her son, her lonely, lonely son, had met a girl, oh how lovely...

"Mom," I said, "it's not what you think. She's not any good. She's one of those kids that hangs out at the Seven Eleven. Tell her I don't want to have anything to do with her. Tell her I'm sick. Tell her anything. Make her go away!"

"But Steven, she came all the way out to see you! You

could at least say hello!"

My mom was still off in her wonderland.

"Mom," I said firmly, "She comes from the Bee Hive!"

"Oh," said my mom, coming back, at last, pressing her lips tightly together. "Oh, son, how dreadful."

My mom went back downstairs and in a little while I heard the car pulling away.

"I'm sorry," I said to Kevin. "That's the way it has to be."

"If you say so, Dad," he said.

My mom didn't ask me about it. She must have thought I'd done something shameful at the Bee Hive, something like what I had done with the sheep years before. The next day at lunch we were all quiet—I knew then that my mom had done what she always did. She had gone to my father about it, and they had held some sort of important conference in the night, and they were worried about their son.

"Pass the potatoes, Steven," said my dad.

The phone rang. My mom went to answer it.

"Steven," she said, "it's for you."

"Tell her I'm not home," I cried.

My arm convulsed, sending a glass of milk flying across the room, smashing against the wall.

"God damn it, Son!" shouted my father. "God damn it all to hell!"

"Please, Mom," I cried, and my knee jerked up and knocked the table. I saw my father's soup spilling onto the cloth.

"What the hell is going on?" my father cried.

"Steven!" yelped my mother. "It's not her! It's a man on the telephone for goodness sake! Get a hold of yourself!"

I calmed down.

"I'm sorry, Mom," I said. "I'm sorry, Dad."

I went over to the wall and started picking up the pieces

of glass.

"Steven! Leave that! There's someone on the phone!"

"Oh, yeah," I said. "Sorry, Mom."

"Hello," I said to the phone.

"Hello, Steven," said the man.

It was the guy from the stationery store. In my mind, though, he wore a big smiling clown face, with a crazy look in his eyes. Then, as he spoke, I realized a funny thing—I was twenty-four years old and this was the first telephone call I had ever received.

"Steven," he said, "I thought I'd give you a call because we've had that ribbon you ordered sitting here for a couple weeks."

"Th-th-thank y-you," I said to the big smiling clown.

The virus had come to my throat and was clawing at the words as I tried to spit them out.

"Th-thank you v-very much."

I put the phone down and went back into the dining room. My mom was sweeping up the glass and my dad was sitting there looking at his spilled soup in disgust.

"What the hell is it, Son?" he said. "Have you gotten involved with some kind of whore? Is that it? For Christ's sake!"

"Robert!" snapped my mother. "Hold your tongue!"

I thought of the big smiling clown holding a typewriter ribbon in his giant hands, a typewriter ribbon which was supposed to fly me away to another universe. And I thought of her, who was me, and how we were supposed to fly away together.

"Steven!" shouted my dad.

"N-no Dad, I d-d-don't even know her, I p-p-promise. Y-y-you don't need to g-get upset!"

They looked at me in horror. I must have seemed like a demented monster. It was like a little time out, then, all of us looking at one another, and for this brief moment the agreement had been broken. I had succumbed. I was displaying my true condition, as truly as it could ever be expressed to them, and they were mortified. Suddenly, all three of our minds communicated in telepathy, at lightning speed, as another agreement was drawn up and agreed to and signed again in blood. This agreement was that we would all pretend we hadn't seen what we had just seen— the demented monster—and as soon as it was signed I stopped acting like an idiot and began talking sensibly.

"It's not what you think."

"Do you owe them money?" demanded my dad. "Is that what it is, Son? Do you owe them money?"

"No, Dad," I said, soberly. "The honest truth is that I never met that girl, but she and some other kids make fun of me sometimes when I go to the store. She was just coming out here as a joke, that's all."

"Who was on the phone, Son?" asked my mom.

"Oh, the phone? That was just the stationery store calling to say my typewriter ribbon had come in."

"Your typewriter ribbon?"

"Yes," I said. "For the typewriter you bought me for Christmas, Mom. The ribbon ran out. I had to order another."

I bent down to help clean up the mess.

RED FOR LIE

Later that night we were watching TV when my dad went over to the set and shut it off in the middle of a show.

"Son," he said, coming over to me. He looked at me gently, touching my shoulder with his hand. "What's going on?"

"What do you mean?" I asked.

"Who was that on the phone today, Son? You don't have to lie to us."

My mother cast her eyes down at the rug. I could tell she'd been up to something—another "conference" had been held.

"It was the stationery store. I told you."

"Son," said my dad, reaching into his cardigan pocket to pull out a little black thing, which I recognized as the ribbon from my Christmas typewriter, "I don't know anything about typewriters, but your mother tells me that this has hardly been used."

"Oh, my God," I said, glaring at my mother, "you've been snooping around my room!"

"I wasn't snooping," my mother lied. "I was cleaning and I noticed it and I remembered what you said, Steven, about the ribbon, and I was confused, that's all. We're not accusing you, but we're confused."

"Who called today, Son?" said my dad. "Was it someone from that... place?"

"It was the stationery store!" I growled. "You can go in and check tomorrow if you want. I ordered a special ribbon for the typewriter, that's all!"

"What's wrong with this ribbon, Son?" asked my dad.

"Nothing's wrong with it! But I ordered a special ribbon. You can call the store if you don't believe me!"

"What kind of special ribbon?" asked my mom. "What are you talking about, Steven?"

"Well!" I said, pausing. "Red ink! One that types in red ink!"

"Oh."

"I don't want any more questions," I declared. "And stay out of my room."

I marched off to bed where I made a plan to go to the stationery store the next day and buy a red ribbon to prove my story. But something happened. Before we sat down to lunch the next day after chores my mother said "Oh, Steven, I picked up your ribbon for you."

"What?"

"I'm sorry I didn't believe you," she went on, rubbing my head. "I went to the store and I picked it up and paid for it for you."

She handed me a package and inside was my lie, unopened.

"Forgive me, Steven," she apologized. "I never should have doubted you."

"It's okay, Mom."

"Are you working on a story?"

"Uh... yes."

I went upstairs with the package. What I found inside was odd. The ribbon was red. My lie turned out to be half-true. Half the ribbon was red, half the ribbon was black.

"Red for lie, black for truth," I said to myself.

I pulled out something from under my bed—something which was half typewriter and half spaceship. I put the ribbon inside the machine. It fit perfectly. Then I closed the cover.

"Let's take it for a spin!" said Kevin.

I knew the half of the typewriter that was a spaceship was the lie half of it, and that it wouldn't really fly. But I put a piece of paper into the machine anyway. Then I typed the word "on." On the piece of paper in black letters was printed the word "on." But nothing else happened.

"The machine is only printing black," I said to Kevin. "But after I remember the secret code it will print in letters that are half black and half red and that's when the machine will turn on."

"Don't you remember the secret code, Dad?"

"No," I said, pushing the machine back under the bed. "I don't remember."

"But you will remember, won't you, Dad?"

"Yes," I said, "I will. Someday..."

THE SECOND VISIT

About a week after I got the ribbon we were sitting at dinner when a car pulled up the driveway again, but this time I wasn't afraid. I had already made up my mind that if she came again I would explain to her that the whole thing was half a lie and I would ask her to stop bothering me.

But it turned out that it wasn't her car. In fact, it was a police car, and when my father answered the door, standing in the door was a policeman who knew him from somewhere.

"Rob," he said, "Mrs. Jones. I'm sorry to bother you folks. May I come in for a second?"

"Sure," said my dad. "Sit down, Tom."

"No thanks," he said, "I won't be long."

"Is something wrong?" asked my mom. She and my dad were huddling around the policeman like basketball players trying to defend their end of the court.

"No, no," said the policeman. "I wouldn't come by except I know you folks and I thought I should let you know."

"Let us know what?" asked my mom, glancing over at me on the couch.

"Well, a girl came into the station and she made out a

complaint against Steven here."

"What!"

"Now that's exactly why I didn't want to come by, Mrs. Jones, because I didn't want to upset anybody, but then I felt you deserved to hear about it at least."

"Hear about what?"

"About her coming in and making the complaint," he said.

I noticed that my parents were both breaking the town agreement, staring right into the policeman's face—they wanted so badly for him to come out and say what he had to say that they were trying with their eyes to decipher what it was before he said it, as if they could find it somewhere in his head if they looked at him hard enough. The policeman, on the other hand, was following the rules to the letter—instead of looking back at my parents he was staring intently down at a little doily sitting on the side table, fingering it with his left hand as though fascinated by its cardboard texture.

"Well," he went on at last, "she's a little crazy, you know. We've had trouble with her in the past so we didn't put much stock into it, of course, but she said Steven had been following her around and was harassing her, or something like that. We really couldn't make too much sense out of it. What she said was that we should ask him to stop bothering her and she didn't explain exactly how he was bothering her, but that was the gist of it. We put her off, you know. We said we'd look into it, and she got a little hepped up and started yelling and, well, we had to practically drag her out of there in the end."

"What girl?" said my mom. "What girl are you talking about?"

"Well, her name is Clara Price," he continued, still looking down at the doily. "Like I mentioned, she's been in for drugs and drunkenness and things like that. We know her pretty well."

"When did she say my son had been bothering her?" demanded my mom, standing up real straight like an angry rooster.

"She didn't say, Ma'am," answered the policeman. "She didn't really make herself clear."

"Steven's a good boy!" said my mom. "He hasn't been out of this house for weeks, and we can testify to that."

"She probably made up the story, Ma'am."

"Yes, she did," pronounced my mom.

My dad stood there with his eyes squinted as though it was all moving too fast for him, he hadn't had time to warm up his engine.

"Would you have some coffee?" he blurted out.

"No thanks, Rob." said the policeman. "I just thought I'd let you know about this thing. I'll be heading back now."

"Thanks for coming all the way out," my dad said feebly, showing him to the door.

My mom looked at me.

"Steven, do you know anything about this?"

"No, mom," I said.

I thought of the virus that had been attacking me, and all the troubles I had imagined for myself because of the way this girl had looked at me. Now she had turned out to be crazy! That's all it was, just a crazy girl looking at me that day in the parking lot, and it didn't mean anything at all.

"No, Mom," I said, "but it all makes sense to me now."

"Well," she said, "it doesn't make too much sense to me."

My dad came back and they both looked at me so seriously that I had to laugh, so overjoyed was I that for the first time in so long I didn't have the slightest desire to shake.

THE THIRD VISIT, PHONE CALLS, A PACKAGE

T hen she started doing weird things.

Since the policeman's visit I had begun waking up every night. Just before dawn I would find myself awake with the most horrible feeling of being all alone.

"Kevin," I'd cry.

"I'm right here, Dad," he'd say.

One night when I called out for him, he wasn't there. I scrambled out of bed in desperation.

"It's alright, Dad," Kev said. "I'm here."

I realized I'd been dreaming, walking in my sleep toward the bedroom window. I looked out the window down into the back yard and I saw her. Clara Price was standing in a patch of light from our back porch light with a bathrobe wrapped around her, as though she, too, had been woken up in the middle of the night. She was staring up at my room. Her hair, which before had been that fake blonde, was now falling down onto her shoulders in the brightest, fieriest-looking red curls I had ever seen. She had dyed her hair!

"What's she doing?" I said, scanning her hands for something, as though I might find an axe there, as though

123

she were about to come upstairs and chop me to pieces.

"It's okay, Dad," said Kevin, trying to calm me down. I was shivering again.

But I only calmed down when I saw how afraid she looked—not as if she were going to come up there and kill me with an axe, but as if she were afraid that someone was going to come down and kill her. That someone was the boy. Even from that distance she was looking through my eyes to Kevin, inside.

"It's okay, Dad," said Kevin.

I took him away from the window.

I heard a car starting up off in the distance. She must have parked down the road. The shaking subsided.

There were phone calls, late at night before we went to bed, when she would hang up on my mother or my father when they picked up the phone. I didn't know for sure, of course, that it was her making those calls. But I almost felt her staring out from the end of the receiver when my mother picked up the phone and nobody answered.

I kept waking up every night, just before dawn, feeling so alone, but always Kevin would appear to comfort me.

The last straw was when she sent the package.

"Steven," said my mom one morning, handing me a parcel the size of a shoe box. "There's a package for you."

Opening the package I was thinking it would be the book about growing soybeans that I had sent away for. I had thought we could make money if we grew soybeans because the market for wheat was glutted that year, but I didn't know how to do it, and nobody in our county grew soybeans, so I had sent away for the book. But it wasn't a book in the mail that day. And there wasn't any time to hide it from my mom when I saw what was inside the package. My mom saw it too and her face turned all green.

The box was full of maggots. The maggots were crawling around something pink. I could just make out something that looked like the pink head of a baby.

"What is it?" cried my mom.

The maggots scampered to the bottom of the box, frightened by the light, revealing a little doll in diapers. On its chest was scrawled in big red letters

STEVEN JONES

THE TINY DEMON BOY

That was what made my dad, when he heard about it in the secret conference he must have had with my mom that night, decide to go over to the Bee Hive and talk to her.

He finished his food, wiped his face, and took off his cardigan. When he put on his blue windbreaker he said, "Well, I'll be back." Then he drove off in the station wagon.

My mom and I watched television. I didn't ask her where he was going. I knew from the heroic way he had buttoned up his windbreaker, and I knew from another thing—instead of warming up the car for the requisite five minutes, my dad had started it and taken right off down the road. In all his heroic courage he had forgotten to warm it up.

"The poor engine," I joked to Kev. "It'll be ruined now."

My mom and I couldn't concentrate on the television show. We were both worried about my dad.

"He's been gone too long," said my mom after a while.

"It's only half an hour."

"It only takes five minutes to get to town," said my mom.

"He'll be okay," I said.

We heard a car coming and we both moved our eyes from the TV to the window, but then we saw its headlights moving past and down the road and we looked back at the TV.

The next car that came was my dad. He came in looking as if he had just won the war.

"It's okay now."

"What happened? What happened?" we asked.

He made us wait until he had taken off his coat, put on his cardigan, untied his shoes and slipped into his slippers before he told us.

"They took her off to the funny farm," he said. "They locked her up."

Then he must have remembered that his own son had been locked up once, because he blushed.

"I mean, they took her to Grandville Oaks."

"Grandville Oaks?"

"Well," he said, sympathizing with the girl now, "I spoke to her mother and her mother was saying about what happened, and it's pretty sad."

"What happened?"

"Well," he said, warming up his mind while we waited in suspense, "she's had a hard time of it, you know. Her father taking off and her brother getting killed. She's been into drugs, I guess."

"Dad!" I said, "why did they take her to the funny farm?"

"She went crazy, Son."

"What kind of crazy?"

"Well," he said again, "she thought she was being chased by some kind of demon or something."

"A demon?"

"Some kind of tiny demon, I guess," he said. "I don't know, Son."

"A tiny demon?"

"A tiny demon boy," he said. "I guess she'd see it at night and it wouldn't let her sleep, and for some reason she thought you had something to do with it, the poor girl."

"A tiny demon boy?"

"But it's okay now?" asked my mom. "She's getting help?"

"Yes," said my dad. "She won't bother us any more."

My mom brought in sausage rolls to celebrate my father's victory, but I wasn't listening to him as he told more about his adventure, going into the Bee Hive and all. I was looking at a tiny little boy.

"Kevin," I said, "what's going on?"

"Nothing, Dad," he answered with a tiny, guilty face.

That night I pretended to go to sleep, which was like playing one of the Impossible Games Kev and I had made up while fishing. Kevin was there watching me. He was like Santa Claus that way—he knows when you're not sleeping, he knows when you're awake. So pretending to be asleep was impossible with Kevin. But I concentrated. I knew I had to play harder than I'd ever played to beat Kevin at this game, to get myself into the impossible state of being asleep and awake at the same time.

"Dad," he peeped after a while, "are you awake?"

I knew it was too early so I answered, "Yes, I'm awake."

I concentrated harder.

"Dad, are you awake?" he asked a while later.

"Yes."

But the third time he asked I didn't say anything. Then I knew I had won the game.

Kevin slipped out of my head. I saw him outside of me for the first time since Dog Odedience School. Through my half-open eyes I watched him floating in front of my face, and he seemed to be muttering something to himself.

"Sixty-nine," I thought I heard him say. "Forty-seven."

He was using the imaginary numbers technique I had taught him myself. With every number he seemed to float further away from me, in his little shorts and his little shirt, defying the law of gravity, and defying other laws as well—my laws, which said it was impossible for him ever to be apart from me, because we were the same person and I was my own father. But there he was, leaving me, on his way out the window, muttering imaginary numbers.

"Four thousand six hundred thirty-eight."

Then he was gone and I felt that feeling that had woken me every night—I felt all alone.

It sank deep into my bones, this loneliness, and made my heart thump and my mind panic as I wondered what exactly he was doing to the poor girl when he had been flying away from me every night.

"Locked up," I remembered my father saying.

Kevin had been in Grandville Oaks. He knew where it was. He would be there in an instant. And I couldn't follow—I remembered what happened to my body when we both left it alone for too long.

"But why?" I wondered. "What's he doing to her?"

THE PROMISE

I didn't know who I was talking to. All my life when I talked in my thoughts I knew who I was talking to. But suddenly when I heard myself think it didn't make sense any more.

"You're thinking to yourself," I said, but I didn't even know who was saying that sentence now that Kevin was no longer listening. Even when I kept secrets from Kevin, thinking things to myself, I knew who I was—I was the person hiding things from Kevin. But now I didn't know who was thinking in my head. It seemed like a bunch of words going around and around, people-less words in sentences being spoken by no one. Words, words, words—a night of words that wouldn't end. They kept going around and around on a carousel, spinning and spinning, and when the light of dawn came in the window I didn't even know who was watching the light until a boy appeared in front of me and finally I remembered who I was. I was the little boy's father.

"Stay away from me," I said.

I didn't want him back. I was afraid of him.

"Dad!"

He floated in front of me with an ashamed face.

"You lied to me," I scolded him. "You kept secrets. We

promised never to keep secrets."

"Dad," he said, "she likes me now."

"You're sick," I said. "You're a little demon child!"

"She likes me to come to her," he said. "She understands now. I've told her about it. She remembers. Look, she wrote a letter!"

He was holding a tiny piece of paper in his little fingers, with little scribbles which I couldn't make out.

"You wrote the letter yourself, demon child!"

"No, Dad!" said Kevin. "Read the letter."

I let him back inside me. It was like holding a magnifying glass up to that piece of paper. Once inside me the words became large enough to read.

"Dear Steven Jones," the letter read, "I know you don't want to see me. Kevin has told me everything. I don't have time to explain because people are watching everywhere in this place. I can't write myself because they have tied down my hands. I can only dictate this quick note to Kevin."

I looked at Kevin skeptically.

"Dad," he said, "read it!"

"I understand if you don't want to see me," the letter continued, "but please let the little boy keep coming. I like him."

"Kevin," I said, "I don't believe it."

"Dad!" he whined.

"I didn't understand him at first," she wrote. "I thought he was trying to hurt me. But I understand now. He was just so small when I first saw him that I thought I was crazy. But now while he's sitting here on my belly and I can feel his little weight pushing down as he writes the letters, I can see his tiny fingernails and I know I'm not going crazy. I could never imagine fingernails so tiny like that. And I could never imagine his tiny little eyelashes either.

And before when he came up and kissed me I felt his breath and I knew I couldn't imagine that either. But most of all, when I fed him, I knew it really happened because afterwards the milk was still there coming out of me. So please let him come. If he stops now I'll forget all these things and I'll think I was imagining him and I am crazy and then I'll have to kill myself because I don't want to be crazy. I don't want to be crazy, Steven Jones. I don't think I'm crazy. Am I? Love, Clara."

I glared inside at Kevin.

"What does she mean, 'when I fed him?'"

"Nothing, Dad," said Kevin.

But I knew what she meant.

"You're making it up," I said. "She didn't feed you."

But there were little white speckles of milk on his little lips.

"She didn't write that letter," I said to him. "You're making it up. You're the red part of the ribbon!"

"It's true, Dad," he whined.

"Why didn't you tell me you were doing this, you red ribbon?"

"You wouldn't let me go, Dad. Don't call me red ribbon."

"But that's what you are, Kevin. I can't trust you any more. You lied."

"I'm sorry, Dad," he said.

"You can't go back there, ever!"

"Okay," he moped.

"I don't like it without you, Kevin!" I said. "I don't like it! Don't leave me."

"I won't, Dad," he said.

The sun was already up and I hadn't been to sleep, but I had to get up and start work. I was so tired driving the tractor that I drove it into the hedge and it almost tipped over.

My dad and Lee Roy had to come help me push it out of the ditch.

"What's gotten into you, boy?" said my dad when we got it out.

"The sun was in my eyes," I said.

After lunch I was too afraid to take a nap, so I watched daytime television, which made even less sense to me than the night-time shows, but it kept me awake at least. I could hardly get my food down at dinner. Thinking about the way Kevin had floated out of me, and back into me, made me feel sick somehow. Afterwards I threw cold water on my face to wake me up and made it through the evening shows by drinking four cups of coffee. Then my parents went to bed while I stayed up watching the late night talk shows, so tired that I didn't see people on the screen any more. I saw worms in suits and dresses, talking to each other in a language I didn't understand.

"Dad," said Kevin. "Go to sleep. I won't leave you, I promise."

But I still didn't trust him. When the shows were over I watched the color bars on the screen and listened to the high-pitched tone. I liked the colors. Soon they were turning into a rainbow. Then I knew I'd made a mistake and had fallen asleep, because it was like a dream, all the colors swirling around to a beautiful, high-pitched melody. Then I didn't know anything.

When my mother woke me in the morning Kevin had gone, and this time he hadn't come back.

"Steven, what are you doing?"

"I'm awake, Mom," I said, and I didn't recognize my own voice.

NOBODY

Since I didn't know who I was any more there were huge gaps in the day when I wasn't anybody at all. I was just this "no-person" driving a tractor, or eating lunch, or saying something to somebody else. I'd find myself in front of the bathroom mirror and I'd think "What am I doing here?" I didn't like what I saw in the mirror.

"I'm Somebody," the person in the mirror said to me. "I'm Somebody. And you know what that means. You're Nobody! I'm Somebody and you're Nobody!"

I began avoiding the upstairs bathroom mirror. I pissed outside in the fields as much as possible, but I had to go in the bathroom to wash, and even if I didn't look at the mirror, I knew that the reflection of me was in there looking out, insinuating. I thought of smashing the mirror, or at least covering the glass, but my parents had to use the bathroom and they liked looking in the mirror and they would think I was crazy if I did anything like that. Eventually I stopped going in there altogether and did everything outside. I washed in the river and I poo-ed in the fields, carrying the toilet paper with the brown stuff back and putting it in the garbage, burying it deep so no one would smell it. But it didn't do any good. I still had to walk past the bathroom, which always reminded me about the "somebody" in the mirror who wasn't me.

Finally I stopped going upstairs. I told my mom I liked sleeping under the stars and took a sleeping bag into the backyard at night. But still, when I lay under the stars I knew the mirror was up in the bathroom and sometimes I imagined it singing a song with a happy face like a clown's: "I'm Somebody, Somebody, Somebody..."

One night I couldn't stand the song any more so I walked clear to the back of our property, half a mile from the house, and I slept by the river. But I could still see the house, with the lights on out back, and I knew the mirror was up there making fun of me—I couldn't block it out of my mind, because it wasn't my mind any more. It was "no-person's" mind. It was cold, and I began shaking again, thinking of "somebody" and knowing I was "nobody." My only hope was tomorrow, and the huge gap that would come, when I would be driving around in the fields, not thinking of anything at all.

The next day the book about soybeans came in the mail. I was confused. I remembered ordering it, but I couldn't see why I had bothered. It seemed pointless now. Soybeans didn't have anything to do with my desperate struggle against the mirror. I left the book on the counter in the kitchen. When my father asked me about it I told him I didn't have time to read about soybeans.

Then one evening my father picked up the book and he started reading it himself, sitting there in the living room, minding his own business, but I began hating him because just like the reflection in the mirror, he seemed to be insinuating something about me, accusing me...

Then another thing came in the mail—a letter from Clara, written on regular paper this time, in her own hand.

Dear Steven Jones,

Thank you for letting him stay with me. I have gotten so much better since he came and they let me do whatever I want to and I have been drawing pictures in the art room and the people like them. They say they think I can go home soon. Kevin misses you and he talks about you a lot. He has told me all of your stories and I think they're great and I think you're a great guy, Steven Jones. Especially for letting him stay with me because I know it must be hard for you alone after being so used to having him around for so long.

I'm getting used to having him around too, of course, and it will be hard for me to let him come back to you, but as soon as they let me out of this place, I promise I will bring him back. Thank you again. And Kevin sends his love.

Mara

That was strange—the way she signed it with her wrong name, as though she was believing all the stories and didn't realize they were all half red, half black. But maybe she did understand, I thought, after reading the letter a few times. It was written in Clara's voice, but signed by Mara, so it seemed to be exactly that—half true and half lie. I read it a few more times. I liked reading it. For the first time in weeks I knew who was thinking. It was Kevin's dad who was reading the letter.

"Kevin's dad," I said to myself. "Kevin's dad."

Maybe I read it too many times. After about the fiftieth read-through the words didn't make sense any more. I tore the letter up.

I felt like nobody again. I ran downstairs and got some scotch tape and ran back upstairs and began piecing the letter back together. I read it ten more times.

"What are you doing, Steven?" asked my dad, knocking on my door. "We gotta bring in that hay."

I hid the letter under the bed with the machine and went out to finish my work.

LOVE, LOVE, LOVE

That afternoon, after reading the letter a bunch more times, I went into the bathroom. I stood there looking at the "Somebody" in my face in the mirror and I wasn't so scared. Then I went back to my room and I wrote a letter to Clara.

Dear Clara

I got your letter and I'm glad you're getting better. You've got to remember, though, that the whole thing is half made up. Don't forget that. Maybe you are just imagining Kevin, maybe you're not. First of all, it's impossible that he came out of me and went to you. And it's impossible that you know my stories or even know the name "Mara" because I have never even spoken to you. But I have your letter right here which proves that you know the name "Mara." So this is the way I figure it. It is half true, but you never should go all the way into the true or all the way into the lie of all this that's happening with me and you.

Now, maybe, if we get ourselves exactly into the middle of the red and the black of it all, something incredible will happen. But you've got to remember that everything I told Kevin about the space machine and the code and even the Impossible Land is half a lie, and it really doesn't mean anything at all. But then again, maybe it does mean something.

137

I know this is confusing. But I liked your letter. I didn't like you at first, Clara, because you looked right through me, but in your two letters you have looked at me and I like the way you do that. If you want to write me some more it's okay.

Love,

Dara

"Dara?" I said to myself, and right away I remembered that Dara was a girl's name. I couldn't be Dara, but it seemed perfect somehow. First of all it rhymed with Mara. And second it had a bit of the name I'd always had for myself which was "Dad." So I figured that in the Impossible Land I was half a girl and half a boy, and that it was right for my name to be Dara. So I put the letter in the mail and sent it off to Grandville Oaks.

"Dara, Dara," teased the Somebody in the mirror.

"Oh, you stupid person," I said to him. "You can never understand that things can be two things at once, and I don't care. I'm not afraid of you. All this time you're been trying to scare me and make fun of me, but when I look at you all I see is a tiny worm."

That shut him up.

"Good," I said, and I went down and picked up the book about soybeans and I started reading it. By the end of the night I had learned all about planting and tending soybeans. I went to the feed store the next day, and with my own money I ordered fifteen sacks of soybean seeds. The man looked at me funny because like I said you weren't supposed to be able to grow soybeans in our area because it was too dry. But a truck came to our house the next day and delivered them, and in a week we had plowed the whole field behind our house, which hadn't been used since I was thirteen and the "sheep episode." We had it all turned over and planted with a crop of seeds that everyone thought couldn't be grown, but I knew things were possible that worms couldn't even imagine, and that if I wanted to I could grow the mightiest crop of soybeans that anybody ever saw.

Dear Dara, she wrote me next

I got your letter and I'm glad that we can be friends. I knew we could. I don't have time to write much today because we're going on a field trip and guess where we're going? The zoo! Kevin is so excited because he remembers the monkeys, and I'm glad that he's gonna get a chance to get out of here for a little while, because even though everyone is nice, it gets a bit boring for him sometimes. So anyhow, think of us there in the zoo and we'll think of you, too. And I know what you meant in your letter. There ain't no Kevin really and there ain't no Grandville Oaks and there ain't no zoo and there ain't no Clara or no Mara, but so what, the monkeys are still gonna be fun.

Love, love, love,

Mara

That letter made me feel so excited, especially the way she wrote "Love, love, love," that I wanted to write her back right away, but I was still worried about her not seeing the half-truth of it all, and I didn't know what to say to make it any clearer than I'd already made it. Then I noticed the story that I'd been working on for the past months depicting my sorry condition. I decided instead of a letter I would send her the story, and maybe then she would understand.

Dear Mara, I wrote

I have been working on a story for a long time, and it hasn't been going so good, but now I understand the story I wanted to write, because it was meant for you, and it couldn't have made too much sense before I met you. But now it makes sense and I'm going to write it to you here.

Then I put in the story.

THE STORY OF MAN A

There was a guy and he thought nothing mattered. People didn't seem remarkable beings to him. They seemed like nothing more than a bunch of ants treading around on an anthill. And the telephone wires that were strung all over the town from pole to pole didn't seem like a remarkable achievement of modern science. They seemed like a bunch of threads spun by spiders. And the cars moving around didn't seem like improvements in transportation, they seemed like great big loads that a bunch of little amoebas were carrying around on their backs—a billion times heavier than their own weight. And the buildings in the town didn't seem like remarkable achievements of modern construction and engineering, they seemed like squirrel holes that little animals called men and women ducked into whenever they were scared. And when he talked to people he saw that nothing he said to them made any difference, and when they looked at him he might as well have been invisible, all they saw was themselves, the little monsters.

Then one day he saw a little kid playing on the side of the road with a stick poking around in a creek playing some sort of game. The little kid was singing to himself in a way that somehow contradicted everything the guy thought because it did seem to matter. That there could be such a little waif of a little kid singing to himself for no reason, with nobody around! It seemed so innocent and perfect. The word he thought of was a word people used in religion and the word was "blessed." It all seemed like a wonderful dance, this little boy singing in perfect time with the rhythm of the grass bending in the wind and the clouds floating above. It was so beautiful that it brought tears to the man's eyes. When the little boy looked up and saw the man the little boy smiled with such a pretty freckled face that the man couldn't help but think the boy was blessed with love and joy and that yes it did matter. It mattered a lot.

The boy said "Why are you crying, mister?"

The man felt embarrassed and he said "I ain't crying. I got something caught in my eye, that's all."

"Oh," said the little boy, and he went back to playing. The man stood there watching him and when the boy got tired of his game the man saw him take off, skipping down the road toward a little farmhouse made of stone, with smoke coming out the chimney and cows lying around in the yard and a dad walking around in big boots in the mud and a mom in the kitchen making sausage rolls and the man started crying again.

The next day the man went back to the farm and he saw the boy walking nearby, up on a hill. The boy was rolling down and squeaking with laughter. The sun was shining and some cows were mooing. Everything was dancing together again in perfect rhythm.

The man hid in some trees and watched for a long time. And the whole time he was watching he was devising an experiment.

"If nothing matters," he thought, "it wouldn't matter if I went up there and choked the boy to death."

But the man couldn't go on with his experiment because something stopped him that day, and he walked home trying to figure out what it was that stopped him.

To help him figure it out he drew himself this diagram.

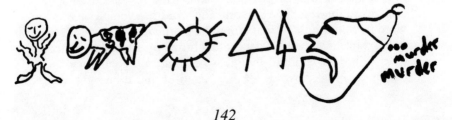

"If the boy is perfect and innocent," he said to himself, "and the cow is perfect and innocent, and the sun is perfect and innocent, then the man watching behind the trees must be perfect and innocent, too, even though he is thinking about murder. It's all connected in the same picture. Either the picture is perfect or it's not perfect. If the murderer ain't perfect, then the boy and the cows and the sun ain't perfect neither."

So he went back there the next day because he knew his experiment would decide whether he was right and nothing mattered, or whether he was wrong and some things did matter, and this time he found the boy up in the woods chasing squirrels and he grabbed the boy from behind so he wouldn't have to see his pretty face and he choked him to death with one hand over the boy's mouth, feeling the moisture from the little boy's little lips, and then he put the boy's body up on his shoulder and took him way up into the hills and he started digging a hole and he got half-finished burying the body when he said to himself, "See, I was right, nothing matters. I ain't even gonna finish burying the kid. It doesn't matter."

So he left the kid half buried, with his little arm and leg sticking up through the dirt, and he went home through the stupid town with all the stupid people and he figured the result of his experiment was definitive and he wouldn't think about "blessed" things any more.

The whole town went into an uproar when they found out the boy was missing. They went searching all over trying to find the missing boy, whose name happened to be Sammy Smith. And after two weeks they found his body and they went crazy and announced a huge reward for anybody who could find the murderer.

The man thought, "Ha, what are they getting so upset about? What's done is done and it doesn't matter. But they think it matters. They think it's so important to find the murderer, but where are they gonna find him and what good would it do anyhow? It ain't gonna bring the boy back. It doesn't matter if they find me. They won't find the murderer. I'm not the murderer."

He drew himself another diagram.

"As weeks go past," he said to himself. "Different things have happened, and I'm not the same person who did the murder two weeks ago. Right now I'm just a guy eating a sausage roll. And in a month I'll be just a guy watching TV. And the three of us are different people. If you want to punish the murderer, you'd have to find Man A. But he's gone already. What do Man B or Man C have to do with the murder? Nothing. The murder had already been done before I even sat down with my sausage roll. I don't know nothing about Man A."

But that night he had a terrible dream where the half-buried boy came to him and pointed with a long finger, saying in a scary voice "You are Man A and you will be Man A for the rest of your life."

The man woke up scared.

"Shoot," he said, "why am I dreaming that? I'm not Man A. I'm Man B."

He went downstairs and tried to eat a sausage roll, but it made him feel sick.

"Alright then," he said, "I'm Man C."

He turned on the television, but it made him feel even sicker.

Finally he prayed to the devil.

"Please, Devil," he said, "make me forget about Man A. Please make me forget who I am!"

The devil didn't appear to the man as he expected, you know, with a red tail and horns. The devil was invisible, and it all happened too fast for the man to notice, but as soon as he had stopped praying, things had changed. He had forgotten who he was. The only problem was that he didn't recognize his house any more. He ran out of the front door because he was scared he'd just broken into someone else's house and he'd get in trouble.

He didn't recognize the town, either. Or any of the people. He ran to the train station, and just as a train was about to pull out he jumped on board and said to the conductor, "Take me away from this town. This is not my town."

The train went from town to town for months and months, but the man didn't recognize any of the places they came to, so he stayed on the train until finally he came to a town which had a good feeling about it. There was a church in the center and nice-looking people, so he got off the train and walked around thinking he'd remember something.

"Hello, Stranger," said the people, and the man knew he'd made a mistake. This wasn't the right town. But the train had already pulled out, he heard it choo-chooing down the tracks. So he had to find someplace to stay for the night before the next train came along. He came to a farm house made of stone and sneaked into the barn, making himself a bed of straw with the cows. But as the sun went down the farmer whose house it was came and shook his shoulders and woke him up.

"Don't sleep in my barn," said the farmer. "If you want a bed for the night, come inside. My wife and I were just sitting down for dinner."

"That's okay," said the man. "I'll move along if you don't want me in your barn. I'll sleep in the train station. I'm taking the next train out of here tomorrow."

But the farmer wouldn't hear of it. He brought the man inside with him for dinner.

"Have some more chicken," the farmer's wife said, passing him a piece.

And the farmer said to his wife, "Darling, this chicken is very tasty. Thank you for cooking this loving meal for your humble husband."

They were so nice. The farmer spoke to his wife with such kindness and respect—the man had never heard that kind of talking before. And the woman served him, a complete stranger, as though he were a king. The man figured he'd better say something too.

"Yes, thank you," he said, feeling foolish. "Thank you for serving this loving chicken to me a humble stranger."

"We have plenty here, humble stranger," said the woman. "There's no reason not to share it."

"You don't have children?" asked the man, and suddenly their faces became all tight. The man thought he'd insulted them, asking about their business.

"I'm sorry," said the man.

Then he saw a tear coming out the corner of the farmer's wife's eye.

"Excuse me," she said, and she rushed out of the kitchen with the dirty dishes.

"I didn't mean nothing," said the man to the farmer.

"It's not your fault," said the farmer. "How could you have known that our only son was murdered just about a year ago this week."

"I'm sorry," said the man. "Murdered. How terrible. Did they find the murderer?"

"What does it matter?" said the farmer. "All we cared about was our son. We pray and pray every night for the good Lord to bring him back to us, but alas, our prayers have not been answered."

"I'm sorry," said the man.

After dinner they led him up to a bedroom and the man was about to go to sleep when from his bed he noticed a tiny little desk by the window and something started bothering him. The man couldn't sleep. He couldn't stop thinking about that desk, and the little drawers. And he couldn't stop imagining what was inside the drawers. Finally he burst out of the bed and charged across the room to the desk, and ripping open the drawers he found all sorts of magical little things—pencils and baseball cards and chewing gum and little books about Paul Bunyan and Paul Revere and the man was almost crying with delight when he noticed the name on the front of one of the notebooks, written in an unsteady cursive writing, so magical and charming did it seem!

Sammy Smith

"Sammy Smith!" exclaimed the man.

Suddenly it all came back to him. He remembered the little boy and the terrible experiment and the search for the body— everything. And then he remembered the devil.

"Damn you, Devil!" the man exclaimed. "I prayed to you to make me forget!"

Suddenly the devil appeared in the room. But he didn't look like the devil with a tail and horns. The devil looked exactly like the man himself, like a reflection in an invisible mirror.

"Yes," said the devil. "I heard your prayers. And I've made you forget for a long time. I've given you a taste of what it's like to forget. But if you want to forget forever, I will have to take your soul. Sign here."

The devil handed the man a contract.

"Forget it," said the man. "I'm sick of you. Go away."

The devil disappeared. The man went back to the bed and lay down, thinking "Tomorrow I'm going to get on that train and I'm going to get out of here. I don't need the devil. I can do it by myself."

But the next morning the farmer asked him over breakfast if the man wouldn't mind helping him mend a fence.

"But I've got a train to catch," said the man.

"Certainly, kind stranger," said the farmer. "We understand."

The man felt guilty then because they had been so nice to him and the eggs and bacon were so good. And after all, he'd murdered their only son.

"Alright," said the man, "I suppose I've got time."

But after they fixed the fence the farmer said "Kind stranger, would you mind helping me milk our gentle cow?"

"Alright," said the man, "I'll help you milk the cow, then I'll rush down to the station and hop on the train."

But after they were done with the milking the farmer's wife said "Oh, kind stranger, would you mind helping me knead the bread?"

"Alright," said the man. "I'll take tomorrow's train."

He helped her with the baking and they all had dinner together again that night, and the next morning the people said to him:

"Kind stranger, we haven't asked your name."

The man said, "Well, to be honest with you, my name is Man A."

They didn't hear him right, though. They thought he'd said his name was "Manny."

"Manny," they said. "That's a nice name."

Then the farmer began talking about all the work he had to do that day, so the man said to himself "Alright, just one more day and then I'm getting out of here."

But a whole week went past, and then a month, and the man got used to life on the farm. Soon he forgot about the train and lived there for years and years with his terrible secret.

"I have to tell them," he would think sometimes. "It's not right. One day I'll have to confess."

But one day the man was driving the farmer's tractor up the steep hill from the dingle and the tractor turned upside down on top of the man, and he was hurt terribly bad.

"Manny has been hurt terribly bad," said the farmer to his wife, as he carried the man up to the bedroom. The farmer's wife brought in boiling water and cloths and they tended to the injured man, who was in a dream, thinking about that little boy he had murdered so long ago, and wishing he could wake up and confess.

"Please!" he prayed to the devil. "Make me wake up! Then you can take my soul. I have to tell them!"

Suddenly he opened his eyes.

"Am I dying?" he said to the farmer and his wife, who were standing above him.

They nodded their heads. "You've been hurt terribly bad, son."

"Son!" he said. "I'm not your son!"

"You've been the best son a man and wife could ask for," said the farmer. "But God is great and will take you to heaven when you die."

"No!" said Man A. "It's the devil's doing. He's the one that brought me here! I'm the wicked man who killed little Sammy Smith in the first place!"

"Sammy Smith?" said the farmer. "Who is that?"

"He's delirious," said the wife. "Poor boy."

The man saw that the people had forgotten their own little boy, and he shuddered to think that the devil had interfered and ruined his confession.

"No!" he cried, jumping out of bed. "Look here!"

He ran over to the little desk and pulled out the little notebooks and other things from the magical little desk.

"Look here," he said, pointing to the cursive writing. "This was your little boy! Sammy Smith!"

"Poor boy," said the farmer, looking down at the notebook. "Come back to bed."

The man looked down at the notebook. Written there in squiggly writing he saw

Manny Smith

"Manny Smith," he thought. "That can't be right."

They put the man back in the bed and he was too tired to fight them any more. He let them hold his hand as all the life went out of him. And just before he died God and the devil appeared before his eyes in the shape of the farmer and his wife, saying in unison "Goodbye my son. All is forgiven. All is one. Rest in peace now, for all your sins are forgiven."

Then the man died a peaceful death with the parents of the child he'd killed all those years ago pressing their lips to his murderous hand.

"*So, Clara,*" I wrote at the end of the story, in my own handwriting, "*I know that it's a gruesome story, but that's the way it is. I think you'll understand it, though, because Kevin must have told you about my problem. I have to stay here with the 'farmers' who are the parents of the child that got killed a long time ago, whose name was really Steven Jones. My punishment is to stay with them forever, until I die, or they die. Then it won't matter any more. But right now it matters and I can't leave. Unless you've got any other ideas. Write me back and tell me what you think.*

"*Love, love, love,*" I said at the end of the letter. "*Steven Jones.*"

MARA'S DREAM

A lot of time passed before she wrote me back. Every day I ran to the mailbox when the mailman drove by, but there was nothing there. I concentrated on my soybeans.

As the sun got hotter the little seeds had sprouted and tiny white threads were poking their heads out of the ground, and I knew something was being born, something between Clara and me. Then one morning I forgot to run for the mail, and only later did I see it sitting there on the counter during lunch, a big envelope addressed to Steven Jones.

I looked at my mother. She must have gotten it out of the box. She looked back at me with a dark face. I jumped up from the table, grabbing the envelope, and ran up the stairs.

"Steven," she called after me, "finish your pie!"

But I was already slamming my door shut and opening the envelope on my bed.

Dear Steven Jones

A few days ago I woke up in the middle of the night and I wanted a glass of water, so I got out of bed and went down the hall to the bathroom and when I opened the door I saw her standing there in front of the sink. I kind of surprised her like. I don't know what she was doing in there just looking in the mirror. It was an angel. As white as coconut cake and soft like that, with creamy, frosted wings and a face as gentle as the Virgin Mary's.

"Ooooo!" she said when she felt the light coming in and saw me at the door.

"Hello," I said to her, and she could see I was a good person so she wasn't afraid. And she spoke to me in a strange language.

"Googliaga, googliaga," she said.

I didn't understand what that meant, and all of a sudden, poof, she vanished. I thought I'd made it up in my head, and I went back to bed with Kevin after I got the glass of water. Soon I was asleep again, but then I heard some weird noises. When I opened my eyes they were all there flying above the bed, about six of these angels.

"Googliaga, googliaga," they were saying to me and they were looking at me as though I was some sort of Martian creature.

"What do you want?" I asked them, and I held Kevin tight to my body because I thought they were gonna take him away from me.

They laughed and all of a sudden they grabbed me and they took my arms off him and I was surprised when I realized it wasn't Kev they were trying to kidnap, it was me.

"Mommy, Mommy," he yelled as they took me flying out the window, and he started trying to fly after us but the angels went too fast. Kev started fading away in the sky and soon we were far away in outer space.

"Googliaga," the angels said, and they sounded nice, like they didn't mean me no harm.

"What about Kevin?" I said.

"Googliaga," they answered.

Soon we came to a strange place where angels took me to a tree house and started taking off my clothes. I felt embarrassed all naked in front of the angels, but I knew by then they weren't gonna rape me or nothing. They sounded too nice when they said this one word, googliaga, and then after they got me undressed they brought out this white dress and finally I understood what googliaga meant.

Googliaga, Steven Jones, in angel language, means wedding.

It was my wedding day!

There was something weird about the dress, though. It didn't feel like normal clothes. It felt like it was alive on my body, and the angels decked me out in jewels that were so shiny they felt alive, too, and I realized that even the tree house was like that—alive like a person! It seemed to be smiling at me with a bashful smile, and that's when I knew it was a boy tree house and he was all embarrassed because he had seen me naked!

Then the angels grabbed me again and they flew me way into a forest where there was a big hall made of trees. Not carved trees, but trees that were alive and had come together to make this clearing in the forest look like a regular banquet hall with a roof of leaves that seemed to be a million tiny little spectators at the same time that they were one roof. And the forest floor was thick with the smell of pine needles, and every pine needle was alive and excited about the upcoming wedding. Music was being played by little bird musicians, and the music was alive, too—these dancing notes were everywhere in the air like in cartoons.

And then I saw you Steven Jones, a big guy with curly red hair and kind of a fat face but a gently looking pair of eyes, and you were wearing your black suit which the kids call your preacher outfit, but it was alive too! It was a person, your suit, a sweet old guy who was happy because he was your grandpa and even though he was dead he was able to see your wedding!

"Hello," you said to me, but you didn't say it like a separate person and you didn't even move your mouth. We were connected and we knew what each other was saying without talking. And then I saw him. Kevin! He was floating above us and you explained to me that he was the child we were gonna have after we got married and that in this place things that are yet to happen have already happened, like the child. He was kind of fading in and out, you know, and finally he disappeared altogether, but I knew he was right there all around us watching, in his shorts and check shirt.

Then we walked up the aisle and stood before the priest who was a really weird-looking guy. He had the face of a man but he had these antlers coming out of his head like a deer's and his body was a horse's body. He got all set to begin the sermon and we were waiting real expectant but when he started speaking what came out of his mouth were animal sounds. I got upset because I didn't understand the animal noises and you told me, "Don't worry, Mara, you'll get it after a while," so I kept on listening to him and after a while I began to get the sense of what he was saying with this braying and squawking. It went something like this:

"And the stars in the sky are not the stars. The stars in the sky are the eyes of the gods, and the eyes of the gods are looking down on us today.

"And the wind in the hills is not the wind. The wind in the hills is the breath of the gods and the breath of the gods is blowing at us today.

"And the rain in the clouds is not the rain. The rain in the clouds is the tears of the gods and the tears of the gods are falling down on us today.

"And today these two children of the gods will mate and dance before the heavens because it pleases the gods to see them mate and dance."

Then the music started again and all kinds of creatures came out of the woods, squirrels and hares and creatures that were half people, half animal, and they all danced around with us in a circle and food was brought out and it was one heck of a party and you and I, Steven Jones, we danced like you couldn't believe and I ain't never felt so happy before in my whole life.

But all of a sudden you started crying and you went off into a corner and you were saying "I can't, I can't."

I went over to you real concerned and I said "What can't you do, Steven Jones? What's troubling you on this beautiful day?"

You told me there was a hole in your chest.

"What are you talking about?" I said, thinking you were being stupid, but then you took off your coat and your shirt and I saw on your chest stuck in with a pin was that last letter you wrote me on your typewriter, with the story of Man A, and then the letter started spinning around and it became a black hole. You couldn't look right through the hole to the other side. It wasn't that kind of a hole. It was a deep dark hole that led to nowhere and all you could see in the hole was the color black. And you looked like this.

"It hurts me, can't you see that?" you whined.

"How can a hole hurt?" I said. "A hole ain't nothing but empty space."

"It hurts all around on the edges of the hole. It hurts me so badly that I'm gonna die!"

I looked and I saw the hole had gotten bigger and now you looked like this.

And pretty soon it was growing so big that the parts of your body around it got all distorted and you were moaning and groaning and you looked more like a hole than a man.

I had to do it. I stuck my hand in the hole then and I pulled out something and guess what? It was Kevin again!

"Ha ha!" he laughed, and the hole shrank away and you were better again.

"Yay," we cried, and we danced around in a circle, just the three of us, and we said "We're the magic family!" And we were! We were the most beautiful family you ever imagined, and love was back in your face, Steven Jones.

"See," I said to you. "It doesn't matter if you have a hole in your chest. It's a magic hole and we're the magic family and I love you."

"Aw," you said, and your face started getting sad again. "But it's all a dream. I mean it's half dream, half real. I want it to be all real."

"It is real," I told you.

"No," you said. "It's only half real. You have to understand..."

And then you started lecturing me just like you did in your letter about how it's all made up and you have to suffer and I have to suffer, and I couldn't stand you any more, I was getting mad.

"Alright," I said. "I can make it all real, if that's what you want."

I looked up at one of the trees and there was a bunch of apples on it, and somehow I thought if I ate one of those magic apples it wouldn't be just a dream and you wouldn't be sad any more and everything would be okay. So I picked off an apple and swallowed it up.

"Mara!" you cried all of a sudden.

And I realized that I was floating away, and that something inside me was taking me away from you, and that was a nasty little worm that had been hiding in the apple.

"Mara, come back!" you said.

"Mommy, Mommy," Kevin cried, but it was no good, the worm was taking me away from the beautiful dream and soon I was back in Grandville Oaks waking up on my bed and the apple had done what I knew it would do. It had made it all real. I looked at the walls and they were real walls and I looked in the mirror in the bathroom and I was all Clara, now, not Mara. And I was separate from the man I loved.

Then it all made sense to me. I know now why I always felt like I missed something since I was a little girl, Steven Jones. I always felt like it was my father who ran off, but now I see that it wasn't him I missed. It was you. I am Mara, and Clara is the worm I ate a long time ago in another dimension. And next week when they let me out of here I'm going to find the potion that kills the worm and then it will be time for you to remember the secret code and we can all go back, but this time you can't be the way you were in my dream. You gotta be strong, Steven Jones, and accept the fact that your parents are worms and there's nothing you can do to help them. They'll be okay without you.

The fact is, you gotta pay a price for everything. If you love me, that's great. But if you're not willing to give anything up for our love, then our love ain't nothing more than a bunch of talk.

But I know it's more than that. Every morning I wake up to it like seeing a miracle, and it's there inside me, this love I have for you, and you feel it too, I know you do. I can't wait to see you again. I'm gonna look right at you Steven Jones and find out if it's just in my imagination, this miracle, or if you really do share it with me. Right at you, baby, and we're gonna have a heck of a time cause Kevin has told me that you don't know nothing about something and I'm gonna show you everything about that something and it's gonna be sweet, you can count on it.

Oh, by the way, I found part of my space suit, I think. So I'm sending it along with this letter just so you can inspect it real good and make sure I'm not mistaken and that it ain't the wrong costume, cause I don't wanta get burned when you take me flying to where you're gonna take me so check it out real good.

Love and sex and dreams,

Mara

Along with the letter was enclosed a pair of white lacy underpants. I held them up to my nose and I smelled her, and I felt as though I was with her and we were all connected just the way she said in the letter. I was right there with her in the hospital for hours and hours as I held her underpants to my face, and I got so excited I started shaking—and then I remembered my parents.

I was scared. I had been so long with the underpants that I had forgotten to go down for dinner. Now it was eleven at night and they would already be in bed. I ran running downstairs with the underpants, out the door and into the barn, where I tried to light them on fire. I held matches to them but they wouldn't burn. I started thinking she was right, this was the space costume. My mind started going all the way over to the lie, the red, outer space, worms, a pair of underpants that wouldn't burn as you flew in them through the galaxies, and I didn't want it to be true, so I found some gasoline and I poured it on the underpants and I lit them on fire and finally they seemed to be burning and at last I was back in a safe place where the underpants were just underpants and I was so relieved that it took me a while to realize that half the barn was burning with them.

THE AGREEMENT

I went running out of the barn to get my parents but my mother was already scrambling off the back porch with her robe half open. She must have woken up first and dashed out of the room before my father, because she had forgotten to tie the robe, and coming toward me I saw my mother's two breasts and the dark patch between her legs underneath the fat hanging down from her belly. Her breasts were hanging down, too, all white and lumpy, and the purple spot around her nipple was bigger than I'd imagined those purple spots should be. Coming toward me with these three new things was an old expression on my mother's face —tightened as though strings were pulling it back and flattening it, and the expression said something to me, without words. It said "Steven, what have you done now?"

I looked at my mother and without speaking implored her: "I'm sorry, Mom. Please don't tell Dad."

Behind us the barn was burning up like a huge, sick birthday cake, long flames lighting the air like fireworks. My dad came rushing out, but he had taken the time to put on his slippers and tie his robe, so I didn't see him the way I saw my mother. Then my mother tied her robe and we stopped looking at each other, and all three of us ran over to the fire.

It was too late. The barn burned down with all our equipment and our three milking cows in it. We couldn't get in there to save them. The firemen came and sprayed water on the barn so the fire wouldn't spread to the sheds.

"What happened? What happened?" everyone said.

"I don't know," I answered. "I smelled smoke and I came running down, but it had already gone up."

"Then we smelled it too," said my mother, and I knew she had granted my request. For once in her life she wasn't going to say anything.

About five in the morning everybody left and it was just the three of us standing there looking at the smoldering pile of black that had once been our barn.

"Well," said my dad, warming up his mind. "Good thing we got the insurance."

I looked over at my mom and we sealed our secret pact. She would say nothing.

"Damn good thing we got the insurance," said my dad again.

When the insurance man showed up at our house the next day to investigate the fire, along with the policeman Tom, I liked him right away. He was going to make everything better, I knew it. He had such a gentle face, but that wasn't what gave me such confidence. It was what he wore—red and black. A red jacket with black pants and a tie that was red and black stripes all twisted together.

"No, folks," he said. "I don't represent the insurance company's interest and I don't represent your interest and I don't represent the police's interest in trying to figure this thing out. I'm just kind of the middle man, you know, and if you'll bear with me, I'm sure everything will work out fine."

"The Middle Man," I said to myself.

The very first day he found the gasoline can in the bottom of the pile and decided it was a case of arson.

"That won't affect your claim, though," he said. "Unless of course you burned it down yourself."

He laughed and my father laughed too, but my mother and I looked at one another nervously. Suddenly we wished we hadn't made the agreement, but it was too late to go back on it now.

The next day while we were standing around with the Middle Man, the policeman Tom, who was digging through the soot of the barn, suddenly shouted: "Well I'll be gosh darned."

With a pair of long tweezer things he pulled from the bottom of the charcoal a pair of white lacy underpants that didn't have a speck of black soot on them.

"How about that?"

He brought them over, hanging them from the tweezers, and said "They're not yours, are they, Ma'am?"

My mother looked at me, then she looked at the policeman, and shook her face angrily as though she were offended.

"Well," said the policeman to the Middle Man. "That just about settles it, don't it?"

The Middle Man frowned and said, "Well, I don't know, Tom."

"Settles what?" I asked.

"It was that girl," said my dad. "Clara Price. She burned down our barn, Son."

"But she's in the hospital!"

The policeman shook his head no. "We've already been over to her house to question her. The night of the fire is the night they let her out of Grandville Oaks."

"Isn't that a coincidence," said my dad, disgustedly.

"But she didn't do it!" I heard myself yelling.

"Well, how do you know that?" asked Tom, looking at

me with a cocked head.

"Uh... She probably did do it!" I blurted out, my voice sounding thin as though I was whistling through a reed. "But how can we prove it?"

Tom said, "Well, those underpants might help, Son. They were probably some kind of sick joke. But we have ways of finding out if they're hers, you know, and we just might have caught her with her pants down, if you know what I mean."

"Oh, good," I said. "Yes, run tests on them."

"We will, Son," said the policeman. "It's a lucky thing they didn't burn up in all those flames. Lucky break I guess."

"What a lucky break!" I said.

I was worried about the Middle Man. He had a puzzled look on his face as he stood there eyeing the underpants.

"Well, we'll see," he said, and he and Tom headed to their cars and drove to town.

THE VINEGAR SHOW

That night I couldn't sleep. I thought of the Middle Man and that puzzled look on his face, as if he were trying to figure out more than just the mystery of the fire. As though he were trying to figure out my whole life. When I looked at that puzzled face in my mind I knew he wanted to help me somehow. There was a real gentleness in him and a suffering because of what he felt for other people's suffering. A love...

Then I remembered. I had known him in the other place, this man who here in the Land of Worms was disguised as an insurance man. In the other place he was no average citizen. He was like a father to us, I think, or an older brother. And he used to move among us silently and gracefully, keeping an eye on things. Yes, that was it, he was an observer and an arbitrator, making sure that a certain balance was kept, an Impossible Balance between all things and creatures in that place. If anything ever went awry, or became extreme, the Middle Man would appear, like magic, and gently bring us back to a kind of middle way. One look at him and we would obey because he was...

No, no, that wasn't right. I was dreaming now, I guessed, because I wasn't in the bedroom any more. I was out of doors, walking across a field filled with people and loud noise and bright lights. A carnival! I could hear merry-go-round music. And I saw an amusement ride in the distance where people were hanging upside down and being spun around above a bottomless pit, screaming with delight, or maybe terror, it was hard to tell which.

A man crooked his finger at me and said "Right this way." He took something from me and handed me a ticket. "Enjoy the show," he said, directing me to a big tent with circus writing on it: "Vinegar Show!"

In the tent I found a group of people gathered around a stage, waiting for the show to begin. "What is a Vinegar Show?" I asked the person standing next to me, but he didn't answer. Suddenly I felt very cold. A chill wind was blowing through the place. My teeth chattered together. "Excuse m-m-m-meee," I asked another person. "Wh-wh-what is a V-v-v-vinnnn—"

I couldn't finish the question because my teeth were chattering so violently now that they started to crumble in my mouth.

"Oh God!" I thought. "My teeth are all falling out!"

I was spitting them out of my mouth, little particles of white teeth all gnashed to bits as I shook in the terrible cold. But then there was heat from nowhere and I stopped shaking. Up on the stage, I saw, they'd lit a fire.

"Thank God!" I thought. "Now it'll warm up in here."

But then I noticed the fire was straw burning beneath a man tied to a post right in the middle of the fire, in the middle of the stage. I walked closer to the stage and saw it was the Middle Man. He was naked, much plumper than I remembered him. There was no belly button on his large belly. His skin was streaked red. There was blood dripping from big gashes on his head.

The crowd was murmuring excitedly now as the flames licked up beneath the Middle Man. I heard loud crackling sounds as the flames burned his flesh. The crowd was cheering happily as clouds of smoke began to pour from the horrible black patches on his body. The flames were up to the height of his head now and I noticed that the Middle Man's hair was a curly red.

Soon the Middle Man was roasted beyond all recognition, completely black, as if he were covered from head to toe with a hideous black armor, juices running from the cracks in it.

The crowd was yelping crazily. "Vinegar! Vinegar!" I heard some female voices shouting. And gangs of young women were rushing toward the blaze and hurling soft objects upon it. Undergarments were streaking and billowing into the flames, which leapt up to consume the lacy things with a snapping sound.

Then everybody was squealing. The Middle Man was moving! The crowd dispersed as he moved away from the post, which crumbled behind him. He was heading toward me.

"No!" I screamed, because I thought he was blaming me somehow for this catastrophe and was coming to punish me. I could see beneath the black plates of armor his body burning bright red inside, like molten rock, molten anger coming at me.

But it wasn't me he was after. It was Clara. She was waiting for the monster somewhere behind me. He walked right past me and found her near the door of the tent. She was wearing all red, a shiny red suit that clung to her body from her feet right up to her neck. She looked longingly at the burning man approaching her, and when he was near enough she threw her arms about him and pressed her body close. Her embrace cracked the black armor, which fluttered away on little puffs of heat. Now he was all aglow with a beautiful rose-petal fire, and she was blackened by contact with him. Globules of heated black liquid were spattering the tent and the floor beneath her as she shifted her arms about the Middle Man. She twined herself around the slippery melted surface of the Middle Man, clinging to him desperately until she had become completely black, and in her oily black face I saw the wildest joy—her red eyes burned with abandon.

Now all around the tent people were entwining. All the girls who'd thrown their underpants were wrapping themselves around young men, ignoring the fire that was spreading all around them. "We'll all be suffocated," I thought as I fell into a coughing fit. But still I didn't run from the tent because I didn't want to miss the next thing, the vinegar, which was strangely at the middle of the middle of this whole mystery of middles. For some reason I was sure the exact significance of the vinegar would be revealed.

But I never learned it. I found myself back in my bedroom, coughing, but I couldn't see any smoke. Then in the open window I noticed a white wisp of it dissipating in the night. I went to the window. She was standing there in her white bathrobe with her dyed red hair, looking up at me, just as she had that night months ago.

"We'll never find the middle of our love, Steven Jones," she said, her voice a whisper right into my ear, though I couldn't see her lips move. "Do you know why not?"

"I don't know," I said to her somehow—my lips didn't move either.

"Because," she said, "our love has no beginning and no ending. It began before the beginning of time. And it will continue long after everything else in the universe has disappeared. But out of the middle of our love there will come a child."

I saw him now—Kevin—tucked inside her robe, suckling at her breast. He stopped suddenly, taking his mouth off her, and looked up at me with a little demonic grin.

"Hi, Dad!" He waved.

He was suckling again when they walked away.

THE LAST VISIT

A few days later we were out at Saturday breakfast. My dad kept wondering about how long we could keep borrowing the neighbor's tractor, and why it was taking so long for the insurance man to bring him a check so we could buy a new tractor. My mother and I concentrated too hard on our eggs and bacon and our secret pact, and the breakfast wasn't much fun at all. I was glad when it was over and we were driving up our driveway.

"Oh no!" cried my mother when we were walking up the front porch.

The front door had been pried open and our house had been broken into while we were out.

My mom started to cry.

"How much can we take? First the fire and now thieves!"

"Stay here!" said my dad.

He went into the house to make sure it was safe.

"It's alright," he said, coming back, his face taking on the hero's look, his shoulders hunching over.

"The TV's still there."

My mom phoned the neighbors. They said they'd seen a girl pulling up in an old car while we were gone.

"Damn her!" said my father, gritting his teeth. "Now

we've got a witness. They can lock her up for good! Don't touch anything. We'll get fingerprints. I'll call Tom."

"Wait!" I cried.

"What?"

"She didn't take anything!" I said.

"We don't know that yet!"

"Let's wait until we find something missing at least," I said, "before we go calling the police."

"What the hell are you talking about?"

"Let's wait, Dad!"

"She burned down the goddamned barn!"

"But we've got the insurance!"

"Robert," said my mom then. "Let's wait. Steven is right. She didn't take anything."

Time stopped again. The three of us stood suspended in our living room—my mother had given our secret away by siding with me so unexpectedly. In an instant I saw my father understanding everything—how I burned down the barn, how my mother knew, and how we were engineering a deception. The three of us had to renegotiate. Silently we were drawing up another contract. My mother and I had the upper hand in the invisible bargaining. My father was drawn into agreeing to something he never would have done if it weren't for the farm and the insurance—he had to sacrifice either his barn or his integrity, and he chose the latter, without hesitation, in a moment out of time.

In a second the agreement was signed and time began again. We had agreed that we wouldn't call the police and that we would pretend that it was because we felt sorry for the poor girl and, in addition, we would pretend my father didn't know what my mother had already been pretending not to know, which was that I had been the arsonist, and with that agreed everything was back to normal.

"Alright," said my father. "I suppose there's no point in

calling Tom if she didn't steal anything."

"Yes," said my mother. "The poor demented girl."

"I'll check upstairs," I said, and it seemed to me that we were the demented ones, standing there conjuring up lies with our minds in the middle of the afternoon.

I went upstairs and I bent down under the bed. The type-writer/space machine was gone. Sitting in its place on the floor was a letter from Clara.

Good Guy

I don't know what came over you to try such a rotten trick and I don't even want to think about it because it makes me sick to see what a coward you've turned out to be. I sent you my underpants out of trust and love and you used them to try to frame me in a stupid attempt to save your little good guy head. But it didn't work, ha! I've got an airtight alibi and I know who really burned down your barn. You're just lucky I didn't show the police your letters and tell them the whole story, how it must have been you who burned down the barn because I gave you those goddamned underpants.

But I didn't tell em cause I don't care about you any more. This is a cosmic divorce, baby, and I'm keeping custody of the brat. That's right. You guessed it. I found the magic potion and as soon as I'm able to figure out your stupid code, I'm outa here and you can kiss Kevin goodbye. And don't you try to be a hero, because Kevin doesn't even want to see you. In fact, he told me the truth about you. Yeah, that's right, I heard about how when you were in Grandville Oaks for jumping off the railroad bridge, your mother brought the doctors the Good Guy doll and they gave you an operation and replaced your brain with Good Guy and they threw your brain in the garbage. Kevin never liked you after that and I don't blame him. He just stuck around waiting for me to show up, but now we're together so screw you sucker. Goodbye and good riddance.

Clara Price to you, you worm

"Anything missing up here?" my mom asked, poking her head through the door.

"No, Mom," I said.

She closed the door, then I read the PS on the letter.

"Have fun with the worms!"

THE IMPOSSIBLE SITUATION

We were on our way to Saturday breakfast again. A lot had happened in a week. The police had closed the case—unsolved arson—and the insurance man was coming that afternoon with the check for the damages. And we had become a very quiet family.

As we were pulling into the restaurant my dad slammed on the brakes without warning. The car buckled down like a bull, my mom flying forward and hitting her head on the dashboard. My dad didn't even ask if she was hurt.

"I can't stand it any more," he yelled, and started pulling out of the parking lot like a criminal in a car chase.

"Robert!" cried my mom.

We were heading out of town. My father wouldn't say anything. He just stared straight ahead as he speeded along, but I knew what he was thinking. He was thinking about the lie and the Impossible Situation I had put him in, by accident, and it was funny, I felt closer to him than ever before, now that he was suffering the impossible. I felt connected.

"We can't afford the loss," my dad said, as though we were right there with him in his head, thinking about the cost of rebuilding the barn and replacing the tractor and the other equipment.

"What about the soybeans?" I ventured.

"Oh blast your soybeans to hell," my dad shouted.

"Hold your tongue," I said, the way my mom would have said it. We were all connected now, it didn't matter who said what.

"We can't afford it," my dad went on. "We'll end up losing the farm."

"We can make do," said my mom. "It'll be alright."

"We'll have to let go of Lee Roy."

"We can't let go of Lee Roy," said my mom, and we were all thinking the same thing, I knew it. We were all seeing a picture of Lee Roy with the babies and his wife.

"Damn you, Steven," said my dad.

And we all thought of me burning down the barn that night, and then lying about it.

"Damn you straight to hell."

"Oh, hold your tongue," I said.

It was impossible to tell who was talking, as though a little bead was jumping from head to head doing the talking for us. It was the Impossible Situation talking through us.

"It was an accident."

"Why didn't he say something before? It's too late now. But before the insurance company might have believed it was an accident."

"It was an accident."

"But it's too late now."

"We can make it."

"We have to lie, though. It's like stealing."

"It's not stealing."

"Yes it is."

"Let's not panic."

"The bank's already breathing down my neck."

My dad pulled the car into a parking lot on the outskirts of town. It was a little church. We had never been to church before.

"It's a private affair," my father had always said about religion.

But now we were approaching a little white church shaped like a Pizza Hut, with a roof that was almost flat, with a plain white cross on top. My father rapped on the door but nobody came.

"No service today," somebody said.

We turned to see a man in what appeared to be a janitor's uniform pushing a broom in our direction down the pavement.

"We just want to go inside and pray for a moment," said my dad. "Can you let us in for a second?"

The janitor saw that we were all three breaking the town agreement, searching his face with our eyes for the answer to my father's request. He looked down at his broom.

"Just for a moment?" he said at last.

"Yes!"

"Well," he said. "I don't see why not."

While the janitor stood there in the doorway like a substitute priest, my parents and I knelt down before an empty altar that was just a big table with a white cloth on it. My dad started sniffing and we knew what he was doing.

"Please, God," he was praying to himself, "forgive me for what I have to do."

In a little while he stopped sniffing and we knew it was time to get up.

"Thank you," my father said to the janitor, and we all shook his hand the way I'd seen people shake the priest's hand at the end of church on their way out.

"Thank you very much," we beamed.

My father looked happier driving home. We didn't say anything. We were all waiting for something and we weren't sure whether it was happening or not. When we got home we sat in front of the television and, finally, the insurance man drove up to our house.

The first bad thing was that he had on a different outfit. It was all red—dark red corduroy pants and a dark red blazer with an orange tie, so that he looked not like the Middle Man any more. He looked more like the devil.

"Well, we're all set," he said, sitting down and pulling some papers out of the briefcase on his lap. He found some kind of statement that my dad had to sign before he took the check, swearing that he wasn't lying about any of the facts of the case. Then he handed my father the pen to sign it with.

I thought of the devil coming to the farmhouse to offer Man A eternal forgetfulness in exchange for his soul.

"Sign right here, Robert," the insurance man said.

My father looked over at me quickly, then at my mother, and we held one last conference outside of time.

"It won't matter. In a few years we will have forgotten it."

"But we'll think of the lie every time we walk past the new barn."

"But God forgives us. We're not really lying. It was an accident. We're just stretching the truth because of extenuating circumstances."

The conversation was over before it had even started. My father was reaching over and grabbing the pen. He looked at me one more time, then touched the pen to the paper and I yelled out "NO!"

My father jumped, scrawling ink on the paper.

"Don't do it, Dad!"

"What's all this," asked the insurance man.

"I burned down the barn," I said. "I did it."

My father leaned back in his chair. My mother sighed. All agreements were off.

"I was trying to burn the underpants," I went on, since nobody else was saying anything, "and some straw caught on fire. I should have known better. But it was those underpants..."

Nobody said anything. I had to keep talking.

"I'm sorry," I said. "I lied about it because it was such an embarrassing thing... being about a pair of lace underpants and all, but they were driving me crazy, so I had to burn them or I thought I would die..."

"Really," said the insurance man, screwing up his face. He was sitting there with his legs pressed together in such an awkward way, with the papers spread on his lap, and something about his face, all pulled back like a turtle into the shell of his skull, seemed funny somehow... And yet the situation was so serious.

"It was all because of an item of ladies' underwear," the insurance man said.

"Yes."

"But it was an accident?"

"He didn't mean to do it," chirped my mom.

"Yes, well," continued the man. "It does complicate matters. We'll have to start the whole investigation over. I'm sorry but... Son, why did you feel you had to burn them in the barn of all places?"

"Well," I said, "I didn't want to start a fire in the house."

"I see."

The insurance man let out a little chuckle. I hadn't expected him to laugh, but it did seem a little funny now, going to the barn to start a fire because I didn't want to start a fire in the house.

"You didn't want to start a fire in the house," he repeated.

Then I knew the Middle Man would find the middle of this Impossible Situation. He wasn't stumped at all. He was laughing!

"Well," he said, "take the check, Robert, and I'll make up a new form. I don't see any reason to contact the police, really. They've closed the case, but I have to make up a new form. You understand."

In a week he was back with a new form for my father to sign. The workmen were already outside putting up a new barn, and a truck was pulling up to our house to unload a brand new tractor. All because my dad had signed a form that told the impossible story of the fire, which, the insurance man had concluded, had been started by a child playing with matches. My father could sign that without feeling he was telling a lie.

That afternoon we took the new tractor driving through the fields, my dad and me. It was the fastest tractor we'd ever seen. It had a little glass hut on top with windshield wipers so you could work the fields in the rain. It even had a radio cassette player! My father and I drove around in that glass hut trying to figure out all the gadgets on the thing, while on the radio my dad's favorite type of music was playing, easy listening. Now it even seemed like a good thing that I had burned down the barn, though my dad couldn't come right out and say it. But we were humming along the grass with easy listening music twinkling across the sky, and in that tractor farming seemed like the most enjoyable thing anybody could ever want to do.

III
PLANS

SOYBEANS

Now that the fire was finally put out in my mind I had time again to worry about the larger question—who I was. But it wasn't the same kind of worrying which before had made me do desperate things like sleeping by the river, afraid of the mirror, because I had my soybeans. They had peeped their little green heads out of the earth now, thousands of tiny soybean plants, and they were all telling me the same thing Kevin used to tell me—that I was their dad. And they were doing something that Kevin had never done: they were growing and changing. The more energetic ones were already twisting and curling up toward the sky in vines, willful adolescents, while others were still low to the ground, fragile-looking infant beans in need of sympathy and attention. Sometimes I thought I was growing with the whole field of beans, connected in this strange process of becoming a crop, a huge green-white-brown family.

I had seen crops growing all my life but they had always been my dad's crops. In the soybean field I was the king, and my dad had to ask me where he should walk and how he should dig when we went weeding them, and which were the good weeds and which were the bad weeds for a crop of soybeans. He seemed to like the way I bossed him around when we were setting up the irrigation pipes for the field during the dry spell. "No, Dad," I'd say, "we gotta put 'em over here," and he'd say he didn't understand why they couldn't be "over there," but I knew he was just giving me a chance to show off my knowledge of soybean farming.

I couldn't think about soybeans all the time, though. Especially at night. At night I had time to think about Clara and Kevin and sometimes I'd look out my window and catch myself doing something stupid—searching for a typewriter in the stars. But it wasn't stupid, I'd argue with myself. Somehow I knew that if they ever got the secret code figured out and the machine started up, and they started flying back to the Impossible Land, it would have to be at night, and that's why I looked for them in the stars. It couldn't be in the daytime. Only in the nighttime would you have that mysterious force that you would need to do something as impossible as that. They would definitely be leaving late at night if they were leaving at all.

Of course I knew they weren't leaving because it was all a half-lie, the whole story of the space machine. At night, though, things that were half true seemed possible, and I couldn't bring myself from the window. I'd sit there thinking maybe they'd already left and I'd missed them. That would be bad. I couldn't go with them, but I deserved at least to be included in it, if only from down here watching through my window. I didn't care if they waved back at me. Just to see them would have been enough. It would have been nice, of course, if they waved, and sometimes I imagined them up there waving and forgiving me for what I had done with the underpants.

That was the worst of it, remembering how nasty Clara had sounded in that last letter, which I had torn up but not forgotten. All those names she called me—coward and Good Guy with my brain thrown in the garbage. I didn't even mind the names so much, it was how mean she had sounded, the same girl who had sounded so different in another letter she had written, telling about her beautiful dream. I felt I had killed the person who had written that beautiful letter, and there was nothing I could do to bring her back.

Whatever happened now, it wouldn't be so good. When we had written those first letters and talked about this mysterious thing we shared, and how scary and amazing it all was, it had been good, the mystery between us. But now it had been separated into two parts and the mystery wasn't the same. Even if another miracle happened and one night I saw her and Kev floating up into the sky and waving goodbye, that would be exciting, but not half as exciting as what had happened at first when we connected, she and I, in the middle of something we didn't understand.

I could understand a typewriter in the stars. It was hard to believe, but it was understandable. Yet when she had looked at me in the Seven Eleven and seen something that was invisible to everyone else, it was impossible to understand. Unless you went all the way into the red part of the story—then you could understand it. But if you stood in the black part of the story where the imagination was just the imagination, then it was impossible to understand how a girl could just look in someone's eyes and see what they were imagining—everything they were imagining, even stories they had forgotten themselves. How could a girl do that? You'd have to call her a psychic or something, and then maybe you could understand it. But then you'd get in trouble, because if the girl was a psychic, why hadn't she figured out the secret code and gone flying into the stars? If you were standing in the black part of the story you knew she wasn't in the stars and never would be and was probably this very minute hanging out in front of the Seven

Eleven doing nothing.

"Well," you might say. "It's possible to read minds. There are people with this power. This is possible. But it is scientifically impossible to fly away on a typewriter. There's only so far you can go with a psychic phenomenon."

Then you'd have it figured out for a while. And you could go to bed. Because it was a stupid thing to watch for shooting typewriters in the night sky. So you'd close the curtain, but you'd know the stars were still up there, and with them, the possibility of a flying typewriter. Then you'd get in bed and turn your back to the window, but it was still there, that window and those stars, and that possible flight. And the very fact that you were thinking about the stars gave you away: you didn't really believe the black part of the story—that the flight was impossible; and yet you didn't really believe the red part of it, either—that the flight was possible. You were stuck in the middle, halfway between fact and fiction, believing nothing. And then the window might as well have been that mirror in the bathroom with the guy saying "I'm somebody," because it was affecting you the same way, and there was no escape.

It was time to start asking yourself a horrible question. If a typewriter in the stars was not possible, then how possible was a person inside a head? Wasn't that just as outrageous? And who'd been doing all this thinking and theorizing? Was it you? Why did the pronoun "you" come into your thinking? Who was you? And where were you? Weren't you floating just as mysteriously through space as that typewriter? Weren't you a figment of your own imagination, stuck in a society of worms? Weren't you, in fact, a worm?

"No," you'd respond. "I'm a person."

But now the window behind the curtain was saying, "*No*

you're not a person. And you're not a worm. You're some kind of mistake lying there on your bed. There's something in your head that doesn't make any sense at all and that something is you. If I were you I'd be worried."

"I'm just tired," you'd say. *"I need to get some sleep."*

"Yes, run away to sleep," the window would say. *"But admit first that you're a coward and you're afraid to ask yourself the only question worth asking."*

"*I am a coward,*" you'd admit, but even then you'd know you were still lying, and it wasn't cowardice at all that kept you from the question. It was survival. There was something in you that would die if you went all the way into the black part of the story. If you went into the black part of the story you had to admit that you were, in fact, the dead Steven Jones, and you'd been dead for years and years and there wasn't any hope of bringing him back to life. No hope at all.

The best thing you could hope for, then, was to shut yourself up and stop worrying and stop talking to yourself, because in the end it didn't matter: red, black, lie, truth. All that really mattered was getting to sleep so you'd have enough energy to do tomorrow's chores. But you couldn't shut yourself up because the machinery had over-evolved. It had become defective, like a vacuum cleaner bought for the simple chore of sucking up dirt on the carpet, which was beginning to turn the hose on itself, trying to suck itself into the bag because it thought it saw dirt somewhere but wasn't exactly sure...

"That's right," the window would say. *"You are dirty."*

You'd think of that tone of voice she had used in her letter and then you'd realize who was talking to you from behind the curtain: it was Clara.

"Ha!" the window would answer in the same mocking tone. *"You give yourself too much credit, buddy. You*

couldn't be me if your life depended on it."

You'd rush to the curtain and pull it back because you were sure she would be there hiding behind it. Just before you got there you'd hear her laugh, but when the curtain opened you would only see the stars, and the cycle would start all over again. "Could there be a typewriter in the stars?" And you hated to ask that question because you knew where it led. In a minute you were bound to be asking yourself who was asking the question. But you asked about a typewriter in the stars because you liked that part of the cycle, it attracted you, and you thought if you tried one more time you might be able to think yourself into a cycle that was better, or maybe you could think your way out of the cycle altogether, and finally be just a person lying on a bed, about to fall asleep, free from all of it.

In the morning when you went out and felt the cool air on your nose you didn't have any doubt about who you were. You were somebody squatting down to check the color of the soybeans. And with the land spread out in all directions from the place you were crouching it seemed you weren't separate from any of it. You were part of it all—not just the crop of beans. You were part of the corn and part of the trees and part of the wind. You were just one tiny part of something much bigger, and for this tiny dot of a particle to go asking itself who it was—that was the stupidest thing you ever heard. It would never happen again! Until later that night, when the land disappeared into the black glove of the night, and night went out walking into the unknown and you found yourself squatting down to inspect something less assuring than a little soybean. You found yourself inspecting the little bean of reality that the night had left behind, the little bean that was nothing but yourself.

HEAVEN

It was a relief when, after two months of the cycle, as the beans grew taller in the late summer and soon would be ready for harvest, the phone finally rang. I knew it was her. I stood up from the breakfast table and answered it myself.

"Hello, Clara."

"Well, now," she said. "Aren't we psychic."

I looked up at my mom and dad. They cast their eyes back down at their food. I walked with the phone toward the living room. It only stretched as far as the doorway.

"I'm sorry, Clara," I muttered, quietly as possible.

"Oh, you don't gotta sound all ashamed of yourself," she said, and for some reason I imagined her on the other end of the phone with hardly anything on. I didn't imagine it, really. I felt it in the way she spoke, as though she were almost naked, and was trying to do something with her voice, trying to let me see her body and feel the way her body was warm and soft, sending me that cloud of something that surrounds a woman that has hardly anything on and is lying perhaps face down on a bed propping herself up on an elbow as she speaks—it all came over the phone, and I felt hard in my pants.

"I don't know why you did it, Steven Jones," she said, and she said my name in a way that I sensed was part of

her plan. She said it to remind me that I was a man—
Steven Jones.

"I'm sure you had your reasons," she went on, and I
thought I felt her moving as she spoke, adjusting her position on whatever she was lying on. Her moving had stirred
up that cloud of womanly electricity around her and now I
saw the strap of a black bra on her shoulder. White and
warm her shoulder felt, in my mind.

"But I forgive you," she said.

"It was an accident," I said.

"I don't believe in accidents," she said.

"Clara..."

"Don't get me wrong," she said, and I felt her shift
again, moving her leg. I could see all her long white leg
and then her underwear, black between her legs.

"I don't want it to be messy, that's all," she went on.
"I've realized it's not your fault and it's not my fault. It's
nobody's fault, so there's no sense in leaving bitterness
between us when I go."

"When you go?" I said, catching my dad's eye looking
up at me from the kitchen. He went back to his food.

"Yeah, we're leaving," she said, and she sounded pitiful
then, both because I knew it was impossible—she wasn't
leaving—and because I didn't detect much enthusiasm in
her voice. Even if she was leaving, she didn't sound too
excited about it.

"It'll be at midnight if you wanna come say goodbye,"
she said.

"Wait—"

"Goodbye, Steven Jones," she said. I heard a click and
the cloud of something sexy disappeared with it.

"Who was that, Son?" asked my dad when I sat down.

"No one," I said.

We didn't have to talk. He knew who it was, and my

mother knew who it was, and I knew she was worrying about it while picking up the dishes, and I knew my dad was worrying about it while he stared into his paper, and they both knew I was worrying about it too. That made it not so bad, the way it had been when we were all worrying about the insurance man.

On the radio in the kitchen came a song they played a lot on the easy listening station, a ragtime tune, with notes that were happy and mischievous sounding as they jumped up and down funny formations in my ear. I suddenly felt elated, and, standing up, found myself grabbing my mom and dancing her around the kitchen in time with the song.

"Oh, Steven," she said, embarrassed as we danced. "You have to be careful."

The ragtime tune slowed down and became sad, and we couldn't dance to it any more.

"Don't worry, Mom," I said, going outside.

The same slow, strange section of the song was still playing in my head as I went back to look at the soybeans. It seemed all the soybeans were listening to that song,— sad and worried too. But only I knew exactly what was sad and worrying about the situation. I thought of the half-lies Clara was believing—the potion that would kill the worm in her and the secret code and the voyage home to the Impossible Land. She had gone all the way into the lie part of the story, forgetting that it didn't really mean anything at all. Something bad would happen—something that would ruin everything.

We had a quiet dinner that night and I watched TV with my folks until about nine, then I said good night. Before I went up to bed they looked at me like a mop and bucket hidden away in some utility closet, they seemed left so far out of the picture.

"Talk to us, Steven," said my mom. "Please."

"There's nothing to talk about, Mom."

"Maybe we can help," said my dad. "Give us a chance, Son."

"She's leaving town," I said. "There's nothing to talk about. Everything will be okay now."

"But Steven," begged my mom, "can't you talk about it? You look so sad."

"It's impossible to talk about it, Mom," I said. "You would never believe me."

"We would, Steven," she said. "We trust you."

"Mom," I said. "Would you believe it if I told you something crazy? That it's possible for pigs to fly or for cows to jump over the moon?"

"Of course not, Son."

"Would you believe it if I told you there was a place where impossible things happen? Where angels fly round and even the trees are talking and everyone is connected with everyone else?"

"That's heaven," she said. "I believe that, yes."

"But religion, the way dad says—it's kind of a private thing, isn't it, Mom?"

"Yes," she said. "Yes, it is."

Then she kissed me on the cheek and hugged me, saying "Oh, Steven. You're a good boy. You are!"

I looked over her back at my dad and we both flushed.

That night I remembered all sorts of stories I had read a long time ago, during my search through the school library for a story about the Impossible Child. I listened to the stories with new ears that night and it dawned on me that there were stories that told about what Clara and I were going through. There were stories about people trying to go all the way into the "lie" of different religions all across history, trying to make them "true." I remembered a story

about a man who sneaked into heaven and stole fire from
the gods, and had to be punished for it. A bird came and
ate his liver. There was a story about a man who descended
into the underworld to bring his beloved back from the
dead, but she blew the whole thing by looking back as they
climbed out from below, even though she knew that was
the one thing they shouldn't do. There was the story about
a man who sneaked into the woods to spy on a cult of
ladies who performed a strange ritual with the god of wine,
but the Furies caught him and tore him to pieces. There
was a story about a man who wanted to fly, but he flew too
close to the sun and got burned. There was a story about a
man who wanted to solve the riddle of the Sphinx, but
ended up marrying his mother as a result and finally poking his own eyes out. There was a story about someone
who tried to climb to heaven on a ladder—I couldn't
remember what his punishment was, but I'm sure it was
something awful. Remembering these stories confirmed
my feeling that Clara was in a lot of trouble if she really
believed she had solved the secret code and was going off
on an impossible flight.

But then I remembered another story, one that came
from a faraway land in the East, where a man sat under a
tree for seven years until he made it to Nirvana and found
out all the impossible things in the universe. He showed
others how to do it, too, by calming their minds, and these
others weren't punished or burned or ripped to pieces and
their livers weren't chewed up and they didn't marry their
own mothers. They managed to escape the Land of Worms,
yet remain at the same time, and they were unbelievably
happy.

Maybe Clara was lucky and she had figured out a way
back, a way into heaven, a secret passageway, something.

Suddenly I was jealous. I was the one who made up the

stories in the first place. It wasn't fair for her to get the reward and leave me stuck here with the worms. But I wanted to be stuck here. And then I felt embarrassed to have equated my stories with the greatest stories of history, thinking anything could ever come of them. But still, I wanted to know. I wanted to see the end of the stories—her punishment or the reward for her insane faith in them.

Another story came to my mind. It was about a man who had such faith in God that when God told him to kill his only child, the man set up a fire and was about to roast the little boy. Just at the last moment God came down and let him off the hook.

"That's what she needs," I thought. "Someone to let her off the hook."

THE BEE HIVE

It was eleven thirty. My parents were asleep by now. I decided I had to dress up in my grandfather's suit, the better to play my role as "God" of all these stories. I put the little silver cufflinks on and stuffed my corncob pipe in my mouth. Walking on tiptoe down the hall I sneaked out the back door with just one look back at the soybeans to give me strength before I walked into town.

The smell of the Bee Hive was the first thing that confused me on my mission of mercy. It smelled exciting and filthy at the same time, like cookies soaked in animal blood. There were two women sitting on the porch, holding cans of beer on their lap. They seemed to know exactly why I'd come.

"Go ahead in," one of them said. "She's upstairs."

I felt suddenly like a man from one of those stories I had been remembering earlier that night, sneaking into heaven or sneaking into hell, I didn't know which, but I knew that I was sneaking and I felt excited and filthy at the same time as I opened the door and began ascending a gnarled, rickety wooden staircase.

The stairs were so steep and musty-smelling that I became dizzy before long, and soon I had the feeling I was climbing down at the same time as up, and I still didn't know heaven from hell. I heard a dog barking and remembered a dog in the story about hell, and I was scared. I stopped halfway up the flight. I decided to go away. I wasn't prepared for this mission. I wasn't up to it, I thought, as I walked back down, but suddenly I felt I was still ascending—I had made some kind of directional error. I turned around again, but it was no use. The stairs had become a kind of maze in which every way is up and there is no going back the way you came.

I reached the top of the stairs and came to a landing. I saw a room lit by a television. On the couch in front of the television I saw a marauder—Kurt, the bearded man with tattoos on his arm who had been my tormentor at the Seven Eleven.

"Up there, Preacher," he said, pointing to the ceiling with a wicked gleam in his eye and an invisible grin which made my blood go cold. How could he know everything about me the way he seemed to know, the way the ladies on the porch had seemed to know? My eyes zoomed in on the tattoo on his forearm. Surrounded in red flames were black letters spelling the word: "Mom." I moved my eyes to his face, which was all lit up with ghostly light from the black and white television flickering in the dark room.

I thought of the man from the East who had sat underneath the tree and calmed his mind until he made it to Nirvana. I tried to calm my own mind that way as I headed up another flight of stairs. The television was playing loud horror-movie music. I had never liked horror movies. They had never scared me—I just got bored. But suddenly I was the main character in a horror movie.

Scrawled on the wall above me on the stairs, in blood-red handwriting I recognized from her letters, I noticed the words:

I KneW YOU'D COME

There was garbage stinking up the stairs—empty beer bottles and hamburger wrappers. A young child cried out somewhere below me. I heard somebody shouting. The house was bubbling over with things I had never known before, desperate things—chaos and decay. It was impossible to calm my mind the way the man from the East had done. I wasn't sitting under a tree. I had gone inside the tree and was surrounded by the horrible force that made the tree grow, the battle of life and death that was being fought in its every screaming molecule. I was stuck in the middle... of the middle.

At the top of the stairs I came to a hallway with a crooked floor sloping down and over to one side. Paint was falling off the dark ceiling in odd-shaped dirty white chips. Cobwebs were hanging on the chips. I saw a tiny black spider in one of the shadows, stuck in the middle of the threads it had spun itself. I smelled something like smoking herbs, and followed the smell toward a door. There was a poster on the door, I saw, when I came to it. A dragon breathing fire.

I pushed the door open. The little crack of yellow light beneath it widened with the opening door, stripping the darkness of the room behind, like a cloth being lifted off a painting I had painted myself but now knew to be a bad painting. I didn't want to see it. But I had to see it.

"Just in time," she said.

She was sitting on a small cot, holding her knees together, staring down at the floor, her face shining in the light of a candle burning beside her on a shelf. I saw smoke from incense burning in a little jar next to a clock radio on her night table which read 11:50. Without looking up she said "And you brought your space suit." She had seen me without seeing me.

"I guess you're coming with us, then," she said.

"No," I answered. "I'm not coming with you."

"Then you came to say goodbye?" she asked, finally looking up at me. "I'm glad."

"Where's Kevin?"

"Don't you see him?"

"No."

"He's right there on the bed."

I followed her glance to a point on the bed. I didn't see him.

"Hello, Kevin," I said.

"Is that the right suit for him to wear?" she asked. "I made it myself."

"Yes, that's the right suit."

"And what about mine?" she asked, standing up from the cot. She was wearing a black T-shirt and a short red skirt. But that wasn't the suit she was asking me about. The suit she was asking me about was underneath. She took off her shirt to show me it, pulling her head out of the hole of the shirt as it came off and swooshing her long hair out of it like a red, swirling comet. Underneath the shirt was a black leather bra.

"Does this look right?" she asked me.

"Yes."

She unzipped the red skirt and showed me some strange black leather costume around her middle, with chains and black straps winding between her legs. But still the suit she was asking about was not this suit. She reached around behind her back and undid the bra, and her red nipples fell out of it. She touched them, fingers encircled by a half dozen silver rings in the shape of snakes and skulls.

"How about this?" she asked. "Is this right?"

"I think so," I answered, with a clot in my throat, my voice emerging strangely onto the scene like a voice from nowhere, as my eyes zeroed in on those fingers on the dark nipples crowning her two breasts like the two volcanoes.

"And this?" she continued, her voice sounding like my own, as though it too came not from her mouth, but from nowhere, from beyond, from oblivion, as she propped her leg up on the cot and started unrolling a silky stocking down her milk-white thigh.

"And this?" she said, unrolling the other stocking.

"And what about this?" she said, unsnapping the chains and straps between her legs and letting the costume fall to the ground, to reveal a flaming patch between her legs. She had dyed this hair red as well, I thought, as I concentrated on it.

"Is this right?"

"Yes."

"But I want to be sure," she said. "I want you to feel it and tell me that you're sure."

She came over to me, naked and conducting heat like a walking flame. I felt it rushing over me, red heat from her hair and white heat from her body, as she placed her warm hand on mine and guided my fingers to that coal that was burning in the center of the flame, between her legs.

"Yes, that feels good."

Then she put her lips to mine and showed me something else, a hot tongue touching my tongue. It felt strange and wet and warm, like the strange, wet warm knob I was kneading with my hand between her legs. With my other hand I touched her flaming hair and I breathed with her dragon's breath and my heart beat with her heart and the hardness in my pants swelled with the knob that was swelling between her thighs in my fingers. We swelled and breathed together. The blood in my veins seemed to be opening up into the blood in her veins. Two rivers were merging and connecting in one elaborate delta, and flowing together toward some unknown sea.

I pressed the hardness in me against her body. She stopped kissing me.

"Oh no you don't," she said.

"Why not?" I asked, and in my madness to get the hardness in me into the swelling opening in her I had forgotten my mission and all my plans to "let her off the hook" and now I wanted only one thing, that the hardness in me be put into the swelling opening in her.

"Not yet," she said. "I don't trust you."

"You can trust me," I said.

I pressed against her, pulling her back to me. I noticed the clock on her table. It said 11:55. And when my eyes came back from the clock they caught something else over by the table. There he was, the little boy, with his right hand over his eyes, and an embarrassed grin on his face.

"I'm not watching," he peeped. "I'm not watching, Dad."

He was wearing a new costume—a silver hood and a silver cape that looked as though it was made of tin foil. In his left hand he was holding a silver tin foil sword. With his right hand he was covering his eyes. I pressed hard against her.

"No," she said, pulling herself away. She began gathering up her things and getting dressed. I stood there entranced by the mysterious femininity that surrounded her, which I had only imagined on the telephone, but which was now revealed to me in all its majesty. It was a dream, a spell. It was so secret, and yet it was being revealed. It was a door that swung wider and wider as I stood there beholding the mystery of her putting on her bra, pulling up her stocking, with a contented look on her face—the keeper of these mysteries, the privileged guardian of this strange, feminine power.

"We don't have time," she said. "Not until we get there."

I looked at that place between her legs and smelled on my fingers the magical scent that had come from there, intoxicating me and demanding that I return there immediately for more of that moist softness I had discovered, more of that fabulous realm...

"I'll do anything," I heard myself announcing. "Anything you want."

"Well," she said, pulling on her skirt. "You can start by telling me the code."

THE CODE

Ilooked at the clock. It said 11:57.

"I thought you had figured out the code," I said, confused. "I thought you were leaving at midnight."

"Of course I am," she said. "I knew you'd come tonight and that exactly at midnight you would remember the code. I knew it."

She finished dressing and came over to me. She held both my hands and looked up at me like the sweetest little girl. For just a moment her hard face opened up and another face looked through. I witnessed the face of all her trusting, innocent, naive faith in my Impossible Story, and at last I began believing it myself.

"So do you remember?" she asked.

I looked at her lips, red and succulent like grapes, and her eyes, twinkling with hope and expectation.

"Yes," I said. "I remember now."

"I knew you would."

"Yay," someone cried and I looked over at the cot at Kevin, all dressed up like a hopeful little space warrior. I noticed how much he had grown these months with Clara. He was about six inches tall now and his belly had grown plump from the... Then I remembered the milk I had seen dried on his lips, and I saw it again, a little dribble of white. I thought of this creature sucking on her nipple and I became jealous. I wanted to suck like him, to be nourished by the mysterious food that was her own body. I wanted to feed on her.

"It's very complicated," I said. "I remember what I did and it will be hard to undo it. It could take ages."

"How long?"

"It could take forever," I said, reluctantly.

"Then do it," she said. "I won't take the potion until you're finished."

"The potion?"

I saw her eyes shift briefly toward the bed. On the night table next to the incense jar I noticed a white plastic cup with a Mickey Mouse cartoon picture on it, which came from the Seven Eleven and was a drink they call a Slurpee. But this was a different flavor Slurpee than they sell at the Seven Eleven. The liquid inside the cup wasn't green like lime or red like cherry or pink like strawberry. It was a shining gold elixir, and I knew this must be the potion that she believed would set her free.

"Where did you find it?" I asked.

"Never you mind," she said. "Now what about the code?"

Her eyes shifted now to a little dressing table across from the bed, where the machine was sitting in front of her mirror. The table was covered with makeup and perfume bottles on the table, and an open jewelry box, displaying earrings with devil faces and necklaces with horns and bracelets that looked like shotgun shells. In front of the box I saw two shiny objects, a pair of silver stars, identical to my cuff links.

"Yeah," she said. "I grabbed a couple on my way here."

I imagined her being flown away by the worm, reaching

out and plucking two tiny stars from the heavens.

"It wasn't a bad trip," she said. "We can get more on our way back. There's plenty of wild stuff out there... Well, you know that, though, don't you?"

She was staring out the one little window now, at the night sky framed there, which twinkled magically, and again my mind began envisioning a typewriter in the stars.

I shifted my eyes from the window back to the table. There on the mirror in front of me I saw something which kept my mind sizzling in unreality. It was a picture she must have drawn herself, but it didn't seem like a picture, it seemed like a photo taken with an impossible camera— so perfectly did it render our faces as I walked with her up an aisle. The "wedding" she had described in her letter was now pictured in front of me. She was dressed in an intricately laced white dress, and I was wearing my black tailcoat. Kevin floated above us, his face a duplicate of my own, only tinier. And around us were strange creatures and trees that were alive, just as she had described in her dream.

"It's nice," I said.

"Yeah," she said. "So what about the machine?"

Confused by the picture and the memory of that place, I began talking enthusiastically about the machine, like a little boy enthused about magic goings-on.

"Well," I began, looking down at the typewriter, "this switch is the important one."

I pointed to a button on the left of the keyboard which had two triangles on top of one another, one triangle red and the other triangle black.

"This switch," I said, "makes the machine write in red or black, whichever one you want. And to get the machine to work you have to write out a code using both the red part of the ribbon and the black, and you have to tell a story in the code, from beginning to end, leaving nothing out. The machine won't work if you skip over anything important to the story.

"Uh huh," she nodded, looking down over my shoulder at the keys, her musky perfume surrounding us like those animals surrounding our wedding in the picture above, adding an impossibly beautiful fragrance to the atmosphere as I rambled on.

"And you have to tell the story so it's exactly true to what happened and exactly false as well, so that the whole thing is half a lie and half a truth—impossible but possible at the same time, so that it could convince the most skeptical listener that what you're telling is what really did and didn't happen."

"And then what?"

"When you're finished with the story," I continued, "—if you've told it right—the machine will be transformed into what it isn't."

"What it isn't?"

"Because right now it isn't a Space Machine. It's just a typewriter."

"Uh huh."

"But even that it's a typewriter is a miracle."

"A miracle."

"Because it could be nothing at all. We could be standing here staring at this very same machine and we might not see it at all."

"I don't get you."

"But we're staring at a typewriter, and that's because there's a power in us which lets things be what they are."

"Yeah."

"But there's another power," I said. "Which lets things be what they aren't."

"What power is that?" she said, and I saw her eyes

glancing down at a little devil face on one of the earrings in the jewelry box.

"The code," I said. "The code will tell a story which reveals both at once—what is and what isn't. And after I enter that code, we'll know whether it's worked or not."

"How will we know?"

"Because then that machine will type letters that will be half of each—half red and half black. And then we can do whatever we want with the machine."

"I get it," she said. "That's why I had so much trouble."

She opened up a dresser drawer and pulled out a stack of papers.

"I knew it had something to do with that switch," she said, pointing to the button with the red and black triangles. "But I didn't know you had to tell a whole story. I thought it was a regular code."

She showed me what she'd typed, pages which were filled with red letters and black letters that didn't make any sense at first."

"xxxhkljhdkklsj," she had typed. And then the word "ON," over and over again. Then more letters: "jsdlkajf9jklj lfjkljkljklrj34jsfhfsjlksdjka," followed by the word "ON," again, and finally angry phrases like "Come on you fucking machine, fly! What the hell is wrong with you!"

There were pages and pages of this kind of writing, nonsense and pleading with the machine, and as she turned the pages with her beautiful fingers, and even though the perfume from her body still surrounded me, the hardness in my pants began softening and I began thinking that everything I had told her about the "power" in the machine was as sad and ridiculous as this nonsensical typing, and suddenly I remembered my mission of mercy.

THE IMPOSSIBLE STORY

Witnessing the incredible faith in my Impossible Story that the pages displayed I thought of the faith of the man who was going to burn his only son because God commanded it. I glanced back at the Slurpee cup with the cartoon figures and golden liquid inside it, and it came to me then that the golden liquid must be some kind of poison.

If you looked carefully at everything that had happened that night you had to agree that it was poison, because if it weren't poison and it really was a magic potion which would dissolve the worm inside her, then something didn't make sense: she hadn't drunk it yet. Why would she wait? There was no reason to wait. When you looked at all the pages and saw how fervently she believed in the story of the machine, how she tried right away to get it started, you had to wonder why she didn't do the same with the potion, whenever and wherever she found it.

I saw a picture in mind of her finding the potion in the middle of some forest, shouting with glee, and putting it hurriedly to her lips and waiting for it to have its effect. But then I saw the real picture. She had found some kind of poison and poured it in a Slurpee cup. And waited for me to come to her room. Because she had a secret.

She didn't really believe any of my story. Even these

pages, with all the nonsense scribbled on them, were a fake, designed to string me along. What she believed in was her own secret story and it had something to do with that golden elixir in the Slurpee cup. And something to do with... killing herself. But why did she need me? Why was she stringing me along, pretending like this?

Then I thought of the man who had such faith in God that he was willing to sacrifice his own son and my mind began rewriting that ancient story. In the rewritten story there is a man who can't stand his own son and wants to kill him. But he feels guilty and afraid. So he imagines that God comes to him and commands him to burn his son. He pretends to agonize over the decision. He wonders if it was really God, or just the Devil in disguise. "It must be God," he decides, and builds a fire to roast the brat. But at the last minute his conscience stops him. He can't kill his own son—so he imagines that God comes and stops him from doing it.

Then I saw Clara's secret: she didn't like the little brat. She didn't like Clara Price. She wanted to kill herself. But she was afraid of killing herself, so she had rewritten my stories to her own liking. The only thing she had changed was poison for potion.

"Poison for potion," I said to myself.

This supposed belief that she had in my story, as demonstrated by the vain attempts to deprogram a "space machine," was really a huge disbelief. And I was merely a pawn in the story of this disbelief. She had chosen me, one day months ago, to play a small supporting role in this morbid story. Perhaps she didn't even know then how the story would end. But she was writing it, and living it, and she was afraid of it. I remembered the night she stared at my window. I remembered the doll she had sent with maggots. I remembered her letters. Then I remembered Kevin.

Suddenly a third possibility presented itself: maybe we were both pawns, and Kevin was the real author. Kevin, who had always seemed so sweet and innocent—or had he? Hadn't he once seemed evil and hadn't I once tried in vain to rid myself of him. Hadn't I once seen him as a sick little worm? I looked over at him on the cot.

"What's wrong, Dad?" he asked in a little bird's voice.

I was lost. I didn't know what was happening, and yet I was sure of one thing—it was poison in the cup. It didn't matter if Kevin had put it there or she had put it there herself, I had to save her from it.

"I won't be able to finish tonight," I said to her, exhausted by my complicated train of thought, as she turned over the final page of her typing.

"But you can start at least," she said, hopefully, and yet now her hope sounded half like deception. I glanced over at the Slurpee cup.

"Yes," I said. "I can start."

She lit herself a cigarette and sat down on the bed. Kevin came over and sat on her lap, looking up at me suspiciously. I wondered if we were really separate now, me and Kev, or whether this too was some sort of delusion. I wondered if, in fact, he hadn't been right with me on that long train of doubt that I had just been riding on. I wondered if he knew I was now conspiring against him, against Clara, against my own stories.

Clara lifted up her shirt then and poked her nipple over the top of her bra, and Kevin turned around and began slurping at her. Turning around to the machine to hide my face I was overcome with disgust.

In my nausea another option presented itself—get up, walk away, go home, ask my parents to take me to the hospital, tell them that...

I saw their dark, worried faces in my mind. That option was impossible. I had to finish what I'd started. I put my hands to the typewriter and began typing.

PLAN A

I worked all night, and as I typed the story with my fingers I formulated a plan of action with my mind which later became known as Plan A. When the sun came up she was lying on top of the covers on the cot, seemingly asleep, as I stood from the typewriter.

"You didn't finish?" I heard her ask in a voice thick with sleep, and sick with something else—the sadness of belief/disbelief in her that went with the sadness in the Slurpee cup.

"No," I said, my voice matching her sadness. "I didn't finish."

"When will you be back?" her sleepy voice wondered.

"Tomorrow night."

"Kevin stays with me," she said.

Then I noticed something that gave me hope. He was curled up there on her breast with his eyes closed, and as far as I could tell he was snoring. Little snorts were popping out of his tiny nostrils. As long as he did that, as long as he slept, it was possible that he and I were separate and he was ignorant of my "plan." There was hope at least that I could carry it forward without him tripping me up. I looked at his little space suit, wrapped around his shorts and shirt, and his tiny sword still curled up in his fingers, but that didn't give me confidence. "It would be just like him," I thought, "to engineer such a complete deception." And I wondered what he was thinking as he lay there, asleep or not asleep.

"Goodbye," I said to her.

I wanted to rush over and hold her and beg her to help me put a stop to this madness, to pin all the blame on the little boy and reveal everything about the "plan" I had formulated during the night as I typed, but I knew from the way she answered that she wouldn't let me near her again.

"Yeah," she said coldly.

She wouldn't let me near her again until I had done what she wanted me to do with the machine. Last night's touching and teasing was as much a lie as any of the lies we shared now. I walked down the stairs which last night had seemed so haunted, but this morning seemed only like stairs in a run-down house. The words scrawled "I knew you'd come" didn't seem like the words of an all-knowing enchantress, but just the scribbling of a sad girl, or a conniving evil, I didn't know which. All the way home I searched for a third "thing" she could be, but no matter where I roamed in my mind I came up with only these two options—sadness or deceit—there was no third.

My mother was up, starting breakfast in the kitchen. I surprised her from the back porch.

"Steven," she said. "Up so early?"

"Yeah, Mom, bright and early."

I made it through breakfast and chores but could hardly hold my head up for lunch, and finally dragged myself up the stairs and went to sleep. When I woke up it was dark. My mother was knocking on my door, telling me to come down for dinner. I did. Then, when we made our way into the living room as usual for television, I announced "I'm going into town. I might be late."

"Oh?" said my mom.

I went up to my room to put on the "space costume"—it felt foolish for the first time since I started wearing it, but it had to be worn.

My parents must have held a "conference" while I was changing. When I came down my father called to me, holding something shiny in his hand.

"Steven," he said, "go ahead and take the car."

I blushed and looked away from my father's serious face as he made this ritual transmission, a little late for us perhaps, but it was finally happening. My father was handing over the keys to his son. Not that I'd ever wanted to drive his car before. I liked walking, so I'd never even got a driver's license. But my father was telling me something and I understood.

"I'll make sure and warm it up first," I said.

"I know you will," he said.

"Be careful," chimed in my mother, interrupting our solemn ritual.

I sat in the car for the required five minutes, watching my parents in front of the television through the living room window, so oblivious to the complexities of my recent adventure. I was glad they had decided it was a simple thing, contenting themselves with the "Steven's first romance" explanation. But it made me more alone with the diabolical intricacies of it all.

The five minutes passed slowly, as though enjoying the impatience they aroused in my mind with every trickling moment. Finally I put the car in reverse, as I'd seen my father do so many Saturdays. I hit the accelerator a little hard, and slammed on the brake a little, but it turned out to be no trickier than driving a tractor, and soon I was pulling into our town's one small slum and parking the car in front of the gray, deteriorating house they called the Bee Hive.

"Hi," I said to the ladies on the porch.

"Go ahead in," one of them said. I picked her out to be Clara's mother from the juicy red lips and the long face she had, as well as the cold eyes that seemed so far away as she exhaled smoke from her long cigarette. She was old and fat, but when she spoke I heard that same womanly authority that came from Clara's voice, and I could see that once the mother had been as desirable as the daughter, and I wondered why her husband had ever deserted her.

"She's upstairs," was all she said.

I walked up to Clara's room. This time I did not pass a message scrawling "I knew you'd come," and I did not see any fresh paint or signs that she had washed it off the wall. In my insecurity I wondered if I had imagined it the night before, or if perhaps she had painted the message not on the wall of the stairs but on the wall of my mind. I remembered those nights when it sometimes seemed as if it were her voice thinking in my head, in thoughts that ran from bad cycles to worse, and I knew the only way to avoid the cycle was to not think at all, because if she could paint on the walls of my mind then she already knew my "plan," and this was unacceptable. I thought of a logical explanation, a paint that could be washed off easily, a child's finger paint that wouldn't leave a mark. Yes, finger paint.

She was there sitting on the bed as before with her arms around her knees, but there was no sexy outfit for me tonight, and no candle burning, just jeans and a T-shirt and light from overhead. The radio was blaring some marauder music.

"Hi," I called over the noise.

"How long is this gonna take," she said, not looking up.

"Not long," I said.

Underneath her T-shirt I noticed a lump then and knew that he was in there sucking.

"Isn't he a little old for that?" I said.

"I read what you wrote," she said, ignoring my question.

The pile of papers I had typed the night before was in a stack next to the typewriter. I hadn't thought to take it home with me. Even though what I was writing was in fact my plan, it didn't matter if she read it. Everything was disguised.

"You're making yourself out to be a big hero," she said, looking over at the papers.

"It only seems that way."

"Well, how do you know if it's working or not?" she said. "How do you know you're not just wasting time?"

"I know," I said.

"Well, I guess it's going okay," she said.

She smiled at me then for the first time and the smile was like rain washing the toughness from her face for just a second, revealing again that gentle, hopeful girl under the surface.

"You think it's okay?" I asked her, embarrassed.

"Yeah, it's okay," she said. Then the rain stopped and the toughness came back and she said, firmly, "So get back to it," and I sat down at the dresser.

"You'll have to turn off that music," I said.

"Don't you like it?"

"No."

"What kind of music do you like?" she asked.

"Easy listening," I said, after a moment's thought. It was the only music that ever played in my life, and yes, I supposed I had grown to like it.

"Jesus," she said, standing up and turning the radio off all of a sudden.

"Are you gonna put me in the story?" she asked, coming over.

"Maybe," I said.

She stubbed her cigarette out on an ashtray on the dresser and looking right at me asserted "You don't know anything about me."

"That's alright," I said. "I know enough."

"Oh you do, huh?" she said. "You big hero."

Looking perturbed she suddenly lifted up her shirt, pulled Kevin off her, put him down on the dresser and stormed out of the room.

"Mommy," Kevin called, climbing down the dresser and scurrying out the door after her like a little monkey. He hadn't taken any notice of me at all.

HER AND KURT

I went on with the "story." It was about midnight when I heard her coming back down the hall toward the room, bursting through the door and announcing: "You gotta go now."

"But the story's going good," I said.

Straggling behind her came Kurt, the tattooed guy in a leather jacket, with silver bullets strapped around his waist, chains hanging off his jeans, and pointy spikes sticking up off his boots. Kevin came scrambling in last, grabbing at his "mother's" feet, but she paid no attention. The tattooed guy almost crushed him under his boot. It was amazing, I thought, that Kevin hadn't been killed yet out in the world but he was quick on his feet and seemed to scamper out of the way just in the nick of time wherever they put their feet.

"The Preacher doesn't have to leave," the tattooed guy said. "It's alright, Preacher. Keep typing."

"I don't want him here," she said, plopping herself down on the cot.

"I'll go," I said, standing up.

"Sit down."

The tattooed guy pushed me back into my chair. Kevin climbed up onto the bed to Clara, but she grabbed him and put him up on the shelf above, snapping "Stay there!"

"Have a drink, Preacher," said the tattooed guy, holding up a bottle.

"No thanks."

"Go on," he said.

I took the bottle. It was whiskey. I remembered the last time I'd drunk whiskey, when I was eleven, and how sick it had made me. I lifted the bottle to my mouth, but didn't let any of the liquid go in.

"That's good," he said.

Then he started stroking Clara's hair.

"Ain't she something?" he said. "Ain't she the most beautiful woman in the whole county?"

Clara didn't say anything. She looked at me with a kind of smile curled somewhere around her lips.

"Take off your shirt, honey," he said.

"He's already seen me. It's no big deal." Then she said to me, "He's the stupidest guy in the whole county," and I was embarrassed at how she said it. It seemed so nice of her to talk to me like that, as a confidant. I felt shyness all over my head and back, and pushed myself back from her in the chair, avoiding her eyes, hoping she would take them off me, but she kept looking at me with this kind of smile, as the guy started grabbing at her, trying to pull her shirt up. She kept pulling it down, but finally her eyes glowed at me as she let him pull the shirt all the way off her head.

"Ain't they nice, Preacher?" he said, touching her breasts the way I had touched them the night before. I looked up at Kevin, who was standing on the shelf holding his hands over his eyes, mumbling something to himself.

"Show him your pussy, honey," said the guy, grabbing at the button of her jeans. "Show him how you dyed it."

"Have you ever seen such a stupid jerk in all your life?" she said to me, grabbing his tattooed arm away from her waist. Suddenly he did seem stupid, like a drunken man in a gutter, the way he reached for her—like a stupid little kid.

"But he's my best friend, aren't you, Kurt?" she said to him, pushing his hand away from her pants.

"That's right, honey," he said, in a drunken slur. "But show the Preacher your pussy, please show him."

"The Preacher's seen my pussy," she said, standing up and pulling off her jeans. "Haven't you, Preacher?"

"Yes."

"The Preacher doesn't care about my pussy," she said. "He only cares about my soul."

Then she laughed and Kurt laughed with her.

"Oh, but honey," he laughed, yanking her down onto the cot, "we gotta show the Preacher what he's missing. Let's show him!"

"I thought you had work to do," she said slyly to me as he started fondling her. I turned away and went back to typing.

"You can go next, Preacher," said Kurt.

"No he can't," I heard her say.

"Oh, baby," said Kurt. "I'll bet the Preacher's never had none in his life. Why won't you let him have some?"

"'Cause," she said, "we're not married yet..."

"Oh..."

Then she was moaning loudly in terrible pleasure. I tried to concentrate on the story, but it was hard, because I was hard, and I wanted to be Kurt. I didn't want to be me and the last thing I was interested in was the story, or "Plan A," so I began turning my head around as I typed, real slowly, as though the slower I turned the less chance of being noticed I had, but when I got turned around she was staring right at me as she moaned.

I didn't turn away. I stayed looking at her with her long

legs hiked way up against her chest and the guy pushing his hard thing in and pulling it out of the red space between her legs, which had opened up like a red flower now, and the guy was putting his hard thing way down inside the flower like a stinger, and pulling it all the way out again, stinging her deep in her body with a terrible pleasure and her face was twisting up and she was yelling "Ohhh, ye-ahhhhh, ohhh," as the stinger went in and out and our eyes kept catching each other, Clara's and mine, and now I realized that it was all her idea—having him do this to her in front of me—even though she pretended that it was his. She was trying to show me something about her "story," and her secret, in a code like this, the same way I was putting my code into the typewriter, and I didn't understand at all what she was trying to say.

I didn't mind not understanding, though, because I liked watching her so privately. It was like she was letting me all the way inside her most private self, and sharing it all with me. And as the stinger kept making her louder and louder in her moaning, it seemed she was being pushed all the way up a hill, and when she got to the top of the hill it wasn't like moaning any more, it was like she was being thrown all the way off the hill and was falling through space, and she screamed and screamed.

Kevin got worried, and cried "Mommy," but there wasn't anything to worry about. She was feeling good.

Then Kurt turned her over on her belly and pushed the stinger into her white behind, he pushed and ground her into the cot, and she made it to the top of the hill again and exploded into a trillion pieces as she fell screaming this time. It was an otherworldly screaming as though it wasn't the stupidest guy in the county who was doing this to her, but God himself who was putting his stinger into her from above.

Soon Kurt finished stinging her, with a grunt. Then he was getting dressed and leaving the room, and I went back to typing. A little while later I felt it on my neck—her hand rubbing me fondly—and I heard some sucking, so I knew she was holding Kevin up to her naked breast. As she stroked my head I finally understood what she was trying to tell me with this whole "coded" event: that she might let people here put their stingers into her but I was the only person she would stroke like this, with this fondness, and she had remained faithful to me this way. She had enjoyed being pushed into from behind so that it touched off a nerve inside her that sent her exploding off the top of a mountain, but she had never enjoyed this part of being with a man.

I started getting carried away with her touching.

In the Impossible Land, I thought as she caressed my shoulder, we had touched each other like this all the time, and this had been the most important part of being together. But when people touched her here she felt she was being touched by worms. And, I continued to myself, she had always thought there was something wrong with her because she didn't like being touched. But now it was plain that it hadn't been her fault at all, she wasn't mean or hateful, she just wasn't meant to be touched by the worms and she wasn't meant to stroke them the way she was stroking me. Oh, how she loved me, I thought. Oh, how she cherished...

Me...

Then she stopped touching me and went back to the cot. But I was still carried away by the coded message I thought I'd received from her heart, and I couldn't type any more. I stood and beamed at her. "I guess that's all for tonight. I'll see you tomorrow!"

"Sure," she muttered.

And all the joy went out of me like light out of a lamp with just one glance from the two painful circles that were her eyes.

MR. BIG SHOT

On the third day I brought something along with me to the Bee Hive, hidden in my coat—a small bottle of whiskey I had found way back in a kitchen cupboard, which must have been ten years old. This was the day I was planning to pour out the golden liquid in the Slurpee cup and replace it with the golden-colored whiskey, just in case my other secret plan didn't work and Clara ended up trying to drink the poison. This was the day of executing "Plan B."

I came in to find her just finishing reading the pages that I had written the night before.

"How'm I doing?" I asked.

"Okay," she said, putting down the pages and plopping herself down on the bed with a cigarette.

"The only thing is," she said, "don't you know you can't kill Kevin?"

"What?" I said.

"Kevin can't be killed," she said, "because he ain't even been born yet."

I looked at Kevin, playing on her bed. He hadn't even said hello to me when I came in. He was playing with some doll that she must have given him, all wrapped up in a little world of his own. Then I looked at the story I had been writing and wondered how she had seen through it so quickly, so carefully had I been disguising my "Plan A," which was not to write a story that would "deprogram" the machine, but to write a story that would make Kevin go away. I had never thought it would "kill" him, but now that she mentioned it, it did seem that "killing" him was my goal, to free Clara from the poison, and then... Yes, it was embarrassing to admit it to myself, I was hoping that in addition to "killing" Kevin, the story would somehow show Clara how much I loved her, not Mara and not any fantasy woman, but Clara herself, and that, because of my story—and this was embarrassing, too—she would like me, Clara Price, this tough girl who looked at me as if she were about to kick me in the stomach most of the time. But this was my burning, most secret desire: that she would give me an answer to a question that the whole story was asking her in a secret, "coded" way. I was afraid to ask her the question myself, so the story was asking it for me, and it was asking her if, instead of drinking the potion and flying away on the typewriter, she would stay here instead, with me, and maybe even live in my house with my parents while we built another house somewhere on our land, and whether or not—and this was the most embarrassing part of all—whether or not she thought she wanted to marry me.

But now she had seen through part of Plan A, and I wondered if she had seen through all of it, and suddenly I was filled with hope. If she had seen through the plan and she knew the question I was asking her with the story, then letting me continue writing it was her way of saying yes! But then, maybe she didn't see the question in the story. Maybe she only saw the part about killing Kevin. Or maybe she saw the question I was asking her with the story, and was still stringing me along.

"If Kevin hasn't been born yet," I said, "then how come you feed him?"

"Oh, we're just playing," she responded. "He's just pretending to be alive, aren't you, Kev?"

"Yes, Mommy."

"Stay here with your daddy," she said then. "He won't hurt you."

She got up and put on her leather jacket.

"Don't leave, Mommy!" Kevin cried.

"Stay here," she said, and she took off out the door.

"Hi, Dad," Kevin said, looking up at me.

"Don't you want to go with your mommy?" I asked him.

"She told me to say here, Dad," he said.

I tried to detect in his little eyes how much Kevin knew about Plan A, how much he didn't know, but all I saw were two tiny eyes that didn't tell me anything at all. I wondered how much he knew about Plan B. There were two alternatives. He either knew about the whiskey bottle hidden in my coat and was staying in the room to prevent me from replacing the poison, or he didn't know anything and was merely obeying his mother's orders. Soon he was back to playing with his doll, ignoring me as I typed my story. Or not ignoring me. But making it impossible to replace the poison in the Slurpee cup with whiskey. I had no choice but to keep typing.

Later that night she appeared at the door again, alone, and she didn't look like herself. Her eyes were all glassy and she had an angry look on her face.

"Mommy!" Kevin cried, running up to her.

"Get away from me you little bastard," she spat. Then she kicked him clear across the room, and he began to wail as only a little baby can wail: "Waaaaahhhhh!"

"Shut up!" she yelled, and he stopped right away, shutting up his eyes, but you could almost hear the wail still inside him, one long "Waaaaahhhhh."

"What are you looking at?" she asked me, because I had stopped typing and was looking at her with alarm.

"I said, don't look at me like that!" she snapped.

Pulling out a cigarette she went over and switched on the radio and turned the volume up high.

"I can't work with that on."

"Go home then," she said, plopping herself down on her bed to smoke, staring up at the ceiling.

"Fine," I said, standing and putting on my tail coat.

"Would you jump in a lake if I asked you to?" she said, meanly.

"No."

"I think you would," she snarled. "Good Guys always do what they're told."

"Don't call me that."

"It's your name, ain't it?" she spat. "Good Guy!"

I turned the volume down on the radio. I could tell now from the way she was taunting me that she didn't really want me to leave.

"Would you cluck like a duck, Good Guy?" she said.

"No."

"Why do you wear those stupid clothes?"

"I like them," I said.

"Mister big shot," she said, still talking up to the ceiling with that far away look in her eye. "You're beyond it all. Everyone's stupid, except you, and you're such a big hero."

"That's not true," I said.

"Yeah, well maybe you're the stupid one. Maybe you missed out on your whole life. Maybe you coulda been President, since you're so smart."

"Maybe."

"But you're nothing," she said. "Nothing at all."

It came to me then that she wasn't really talking about me as much as she was talking about herself, and that this whole exhibit was designed to show me something else about her, and her secret story, and the reason she had chosen me.

"Mister Big Shot," she said again. "Sheep fucker."

I looked at the pages next to the typewriter and remembered that I had written somewhere in there a story about a man who tries to mate with a sheep.

"Sheep fucker, sheep fucker," she said. "Mr. Big Shot is nothing but a sheep fucker."

"Don't say that."

"I'm mean," she said. "Don't you know that? I'm as mean as they come, Sheep Fucker. Don't you know I told everyone today that you tried to fuck a sheep? Do you know what they did? They laughed and laughed. And I told everyone how you watched Kurt fucking me and they laughed some more. You can't imagine how they laughed when I told 'em all about you, sheep fucker. It was a riot. A regular riot. Whatayou think of that?"

"Well," I said. "I don't know your friends, so I don't suppose I care what they think. It doesn't matter."

"No, it doesn't," she said. "That's why I'm mean, because I might as well be. It doesn't make any difference."

"No."

"So what?"

"So what," I agreed.

"Come over here," she said then.

I went over and sat down on the cot. She pulled me back next to her so I was lying down staring up at the paint falling off the ceiling as she spoke.

"You know something," she said, stroking my arm. "All my life I wanted to find you. But now that you're here, you know what?"

"What?"

"It still doesn't make any difference."

"What doesn't?"

"It."

"Why not?"

"'Cause it doesn't," she said.

It was all part of her manipulation, I figured. Perhaps I was being used by her as an experiment, to prove that even the most wonderful fantasy you could imagine, even that would let her down, and that the world was—just like Man A thought—completely meaningless. And that she had to die. She just needed something to help her die, I thought then, because it was such an ugly idea, dying. But using me the way she was using me, she thought it could be done.

"I don't know," she said, stroking my belly now where my coat had opened up, and making me conscious of how fat I was. "Maybe I don't even like you. Do you like me?"

"Yes," I said, summoning up the courage to show her a tiny bit of my secret, because she had played part of her hand with this depressing talking, and I had to answer with part of my own, but not all of it, because it was too early. I had to be strategic, but I couldn't think of any other way to say it so I blurted out: "Yes, I like you. I like you very much."

I felt her arm stiffen on my belly and her fingers grab right into the center, and it seemed like I had not played very well, because she shouted "Oh my God," and pulled her hand away.

"You sack of shit!" she shouted, punching me in the belly. "You lying sack of shit!"

"What?" I said, jumping up off the bed. "What's wrong?"

She stood up and punched me again in the belly. I felt

the wind going out of me.

"Get your fat lying ass outahere," she said, "before I rip your face off!"

"I didn't mean anything," I said. "I'm sorry."

"Get outahere," she screamed. "I'm warning you, I do crazy things when I'm drunk. I've got a gun downstairs. I'll blow your brains out. Get out! Get out! Get out!"

She pushed me into the hall with a look of murder in her eyes.

"You lying sack of shit," she said again. "Don't you ever come near me again, you hear? Ever!"

She slammed the door on me and turned up the radio real loud, but I heard her punching at the wall and calling me all kinds of disgusting names, under the music. I stood there like an idiot, listening to her shout about the things she was going to do to me as she threw things around in the room, and when she started shouting about the things she was going to do to my private parts I got scared, and when she said about the things she was going to do to my parents, I turned and ran down the stairs and out into the street, where, without warming up the car, I drove home as fast as I could.

ARTISTS AT WORK

The next day after lunch I headed back into town in the station wagon. I had the whiskey bottle in my coat pocket again. As I drove I wasn't thinking about Plan A any more—the strategy of getting her to marry me. I was thinking only about Plan B—the strategy of replacing the potion. Plan A was off.

And Plan B wasn't looking good either, since she had told me not to come near her ever again. I had to think of some way of getting into her room long enough to do what I had to do with the whiskey, but it was hard. Even though I had thought about it all night I still didn't understand why she had gotten so mad at me. She wasn't making sense any more. All night I had played the scene over and over in my mind, her hand on my belly suddenly going stiff as I told her that I liked her, and then her punching me and yelling the horrible things. No matter how I played it, it seemed like she was overreacting, and my only hope was that she'd have gotten over it when she sobered up. My only strategy was hope.

When I got to her front porch, her mother said "She's not home."

A strategy at last!

"Oh," I said. "Where is she?"

"Dunno," said the woman. "Why don't you wait a while. Maybe she'll come back."

"Yeah," I said. "Maybe I'll wait for her upstairs."

"You can wait down here," said the woman. "How's your dad?"

"My dad?" I said, remembering about my dad and her husband drinking together. "He's okay."

"He used to be a drunk."

"He doesn't drink any more," I said. "Are you sure I can't go up? She wouldn't mind. She leaves me alone up there sometimes."

"My husband didn't sober up," said the woman. "He's dead now."

"Dead?"

"As a doornail. She's dead, too."

"Who?"

"The woman he left me for," she said, and I remembered about her husband running off with the barmaid.

"Car crash," said the woman next to Clara's mom.

"This is my sister, Doris," said Clara's mom.

"How long have you been preaching?" Doris asked, then she chuckled and Clara's mother chuckled too.

"My son told me you were a preacher," Doris said, when she saw I wasn't laughing.

"I'm not a preacher," I said.

"You're not?" said Doris. "That's what Kurt told me. He said you were a preacher."

"Kurt?" I said, thinking of the tattooed guy and what he'd done with Clara. "Kurt is your son?"

I looked at Doris, then I looked at her sister, Clara's mom. Then they both chuckled at the way I was looking at them.

"Kurt's a good boy," said Clara's mom, "isn't he Doris?"

"Oh, yeah," Doris laughed. "He's a good boy."

Then they both laughed some more.

"Maybe I'd better wait upstairs," I said. "I don't wanna be a bother."

"What's the matter, Preacher?" Doris asked then, looking at me with a cold, mean stare. "Don't you like my son?"

"No, I like him," I said.

"Kurt's a good boy," she said, flashing her crooked teeth at me.

"I'll come back later," I said. "But I left something upstairs. Maybe I could just go up and get it. Then I'll come back later."

"That's okay, Preacher," said Clara's mom. "You can stay down here with us. She'll be back soon."

I sat on the porch steps.

"Steven Jones," Clara's mom asked me after a while. "What are you up to, anyway?"

"Nothing," I said.

"Clara's all I got left now, you know that," she said. "You two aren't doing anything funny up there, are ya now?"

"No," I said. "We're not doing anything."

"Why do you wear them clothes if you ain't a preacher?"

"They're my grandfather's clothes," I said, as if that explained anything.

"You been in the nuthouse, ain't ya?" she said.

"Yes," I admitted. "But I'm better now."

"You tried to kill yourself."

"No," I said. "It was an accident."

"Clara tried to kill herself once," she said. "She's not right in the head. Why don't you stay away from here, boy? Leave her alone."

"She tried to kill herself?" I said.

"She drank a pint of Drano years back, after her daddy left."

I thought of the potion in the Slurpee cup.

"I'll leave her alone," I said. "Just let me go get what I left up there and I'll never come back here again, I promise."

"Hold your horses, boy," she said. "Here she comes."

A motorcycle was driving up. It was the other tattooed guy from the Seven Eleven, Clara behind him with her hands around his waist. The motorcycle stopped. Clara got off, gave him a kiss on the lips and said, "Thanks, Ernie." Then Ernie took off on the motorcycle and Clara came up to the porch.

"Hi there," she said to me. "Ready to go to work?"

I didn't say anything. She was looking at me as brightly as she'd ever looked at me, as though saying with her cheerfulness that last night was forgotten and we were back to normal.

"Where the hell you been?" asked her mother.

"I told you," she said. "I went to Grandville with Ernie."

"What for?"

"Something," said Clara, then she took me by the hand and said, "Come on, Preacher," and we headed up into the house as her mother sat there shaking her head.

"The story's almost done," she said when we got up to the room and I looked at the papers next to the machine.

"You read it?" I asked, and suddenly both Plan A and Plan B were alive again, with my whiskey bottle jiggling in my left pocket and my heart filling up with love and hope, which, if it weren't for the brightness in her face, I would have thought impossible.

"What do you think?" I asked her.

"Well," she said, her face still not darkening, "you got it all wrong."

"Wrong?"

"You wanna know something, Steven Jones?" she said, lighting up a cigarette. "I didn't see Kevin at all that first time behind the Seven Eleven. I didn't see nothing at all. I looked at your face and that's what I saw. Nobody home, just like somebody else's face."

She took a long draw on her cigarette.

"Just like my face," she went on. "It was just like looking in the mirror, looking at your face. And the day I came over to your house, I just wanted to look at you again to see if it was true, that there was someone else like me. But you were too chicken to even come to the door. And that's when Kevin started coming after me, because he knew you never would. He came to me every night in a dream and he had your face, only tinier, and at first I could wake up from the dream and he'd be gone, but after a while he'd still be there even when I woke up, he'd be staring at me through that window."

She gestured to the window and took another draw.

"So I started sleeping downstairs and he'd come to the downstairs window as soon as I fell asleep. Then I'd sleep at Ernie's house, but he'd come and look through Ernie's window, and he'd hide his eyes whenever we did it, you know, and finally I went to the police because I couldn't stand it any more, I thought I could get you to stop sending him if I sicked the cops on you. I didn't want them to hurt you. I didn't want to go to them. I hate the cops, but I thought I could use 'em to make you stop but it didn't work. He kept coming. One night I chased Kevin all the way out to your house and I saw him float into your window so I knew I wasn't going crazy, that it was you who was responsible. So finally I had to send the doll, to scare you and get you to stop sending him. But even that didn't do any good, he came to me while I was really stoned at a party and I thought I had taken some bad drugs, I was so paranoid, so I asked my mom to take me to the hospital and in the hospital they gave me a drug that made me relaxed and happy like I'd never been before, so happy that I didn't bother trying to scare him away. That's all I had to do before, you know, yell at him a little and he'd go away for a while. But after I got shot up with that drug, I just laughed at him when he showed up and let him come and suck at me and I began liking him, he was so funny all of a sudden."

She put out her cigarette in the ashtray and lit another one.

"And I didn't write that first letter," she said. "Kevin forged that one. You were right. He's a little trickster. He looks like a kid but he's older than the devil and he's always trying to play tricks. That's why I hated him at first. He'd always pop up at the perfect wrong time, just when I was most afraid he would, the little fucker. I mean, he's not the devil— he's just tricky—and he doesn't think he's doing any harm. But he can make you do stupid things, like jumping off bridges. He doesn't mean it, though, do you Kev?"

"No, Mommy," he said, not looking up from his dolls.

"That's why your life is so messed up, Steven Jones," she said. "Because you didn't know how to handle him. You spoiled the little brat 'cause you're a man and you don't know how to take care of children. I mean you gotta be nice to 'em sometimes but they need discipline, too. You couldn't do it because really, you're just like him, aren't you? A tricky little guy."

"What are you talking about?"

"I mean, I was pretty mad last night when I saw how you had been tricking me all this time. But then I thought of Kevin and I realized that you were just like him. A trickster. I remembered what my mom always used to say about people. 'Apples don't fall far from the tree,' she used to say, especially when I started going out and getting rowdy, just like my dad used to do. 'Apples don't fall far from the tree,' she'd say. So how could you be any different from Kevin? I figured. And I said to myself, 'Well, apples might not fall very far from the tree, but I can handle Kevin, so I can handle Steven Jones. No problem.'"

She looked at me with a mischievous smile.

"You might think you're up to something, Steven Jones," she said, sitting down on the cot. "But I've got news for you. I do see through you. But I'm not mad any more. As a matter of fact, I'm just starting to like you. I like you so much that I'm not even going out tonight. I'm gonna stay right here with you and watch you work, because I like watching an artist at work, especially a great artist like you. An artist of deception."

"I don't understand."

"Don't you? Well, I understand, so I guess that means I'm winning, don't it?"

She smoked and watched me for a whole afternoon. I felt the weight of the whiskey bottle inside my coat and was sure that she knew it was there. Yet she hadn't come right out and said anything. So I typed. And I waited. And at eight o'clock she sent me into deeper confusion by jumping up suddenly and announcing, "I'm going to McDonald's."

"You're going out?"

"Yes," she said. "I'm hungry. Aren't you?"

"No, I'll just stay here working," I said.

"Do you want me to bring back something?"

"Sure," I said.

"Whatayou want? A big Mac? Fries? Coke?"

"Yes," I said. "That'd be fine."

"Got any money?"

"Yes," I said, handing her a twenty-dollar bill.

"Twenty dollars," she said. "I guess farmers do alright."

"My father gives me an allowance," I said. "But I never spend it. I have eight thousand dollars in twenties in my desk drawer."

I was trying to give her another hint about Plan A, about us living together, about all those embarrassing things I was thinking... And she took it, but she twisted it into another victory for her story.

"Kevin, you little bastard," she said. "Why didn't you tell me he had a stash. Me and Kurt coulda bought that harley we been looking at all these months."

I didn't know what a "harley" was, but I imagined her breaking into my house and stealing my money, and living in a "harley" by the water with the tattooed guy, and him pushing into her every night and her screaming with pleasure and me left entirely out of the picture, and it made the other thing I'd been imagining—Clara and me sitting at the bank with my money, trying to get a loan to build our house—seem like a stupid, hopeless thing. Her hand on mine, us sitting together in a bank, feeling nervous—it was impossible. That picture went away.

"Come on, Kev," she said.

He scurried out the door after her.

"A setup," I thought, taking out the whiskey bottle from my coat. It seemed too easy. I waited for a while. She didn't come back. I checked the door but she wasn't watching from the hall.

At last I went over to the Slurpee cup and poured the golden liquid out the window into the garbage-filled back lot. Then I replaced it with the whiskey, which seemed a little brighter gold than the "potion," but the color didn't worry me. What worried me was how easy she had made it for me, after all that talk about how she saw through me and was onto my deception. And even though Plan B was firmly in place I felt the need for further insurance. I sat down at the dresser and studied the machine.

I remembered the insurance man, dressed in red and black, who made everything alright after I had burned down the barn. I stared at the red and black ribbon on the typewriter. Then it came to me—Plan C. I looked at the typewriter ribbon and I could't imagine why I hadn't thought of it before.

NOW OR NEVER

I had never eaten McDonald's food before. The only restaurant I'd been to was Deason's. My mother had told me McDonald's wasn't healthy, but when Clara brought me back the Big Mac and fries, I thought it was about the best food I'd ever tasted.

"You like to eat, huh?" she said.

I looked down at my belly. I thought of Kurt's lean, muscular body as he pushed into her on the bed the other night, and the picture of me and Clara living together, sharing a bed, seemed even more absurd in the face of my fatness. I put down the hamburger and felt ill.

"Oh, finish your food," she said. "I didn't mean nothing."

"I'm fat," I said.

"You're not that fat," she said. "It's okay."

But I didn't eat any more of the burger.

"Soybeans," I said to myself. "I'm only going to eat soybeans from now on."

I thought of the soybeans in the field, all ripe and ready to be brought in. Tomorrow morning my dad and I would harvest them and we would truck them into Grandville to sell them, and all the farmers who knew my father would be so impressed, since they had all said it couldn't be done.

"A real chip off the old block," they'd say.

But I'd save a half ton or so, enough to begin a whole new diet of soybeans, and I would lift weights and become as lean and muscular as that tattooed idiot. But then I thought of the size of his "stinger" and I wondered how I could improve my own chubby little thing. I thought there must be something you could do, and I made up my mind to go to the library and do research.

Later, while I was back to typing, Clara took out a drawing pad and was sitting there on the cot drawing a big portrait of my face, and from time to time I would glance back and notice how handsome she was making me in the picture. I imagined that she was trying to tell me something with the picture, that my handsome face made up for the other things, and I felt better. I got so into typing then that I didn't look at the drawing for a while. But when I was worn out, and said I had to stop for the night, I noticed the rest of the drawing. Under my face on the paper she had drawn my body as a little tube with segments. She had given my face the body of a worm.

I pretended not to notice and began putting on my tail coat, ready to leave.

"You can stay here tonight," she said. "You don't have to go home."

"I have to go home," I said, thinking of the soybeans, and how we had to bring them in tomorrow morning.

"No you don't," she said. "Stay with me."

She put down her drawing and did what she knew would keep me there. She took off her clothes and got into the bed.

"Stay with me," she said.

"I'd have to call."

"We ain't got a phone."

"I'll go to the gas station."

"No," she said. "Come in here with me."

"My parents are expecting me back. There's no reason to worry them."

"Let 'em sweat a little," she said. "It won't hurt 'em."

"No," I said, looking at her naked shoulders emerging from the covers. "I'll go down and call."

"Good guy."

"I'll be right back."

"No," she said. "It's now or never."

I stood there eyeing her long body outlined by the white sheet she slept in, and the red hair falling down onto her shoulders.

"Go ahead. Get undressed."

I took off my grandfather's suit and lay it neatly on her chair. I felt embarrassed as I undid my shirt, standing there with the candle spreading a huge patch of light over my fatness.

I looked up at Kevin. He was standing there on the end of her bed, holding his doll and looking at me with a mocking grin.

"Don't be ashamed," she said. "You are what you are."

So I got under the sheet with her, and what happened cured my obesity better than any wonder diet could ever do. She touched me all over my body as though it was exactly what it was, nothing more, nothing less, and suddenly I wasn't fat any more, I was just "what I was." Then we did what I can't describe because it was impossibly wonderful and new to me. I didn't have time to take any notice of it. It just happened.

We mated.

"Because it pleases the gods to see them mate and dance," I remembered.

Afterwards we touched each other's hair with affection. We even giggled a little.

Kevin was still standing on the end of the cot playing with his doll, taking no notice of us. Still, I wondered what he was thinking. He couldn't have been unaware of my mind now, racing unembarrassed into Plan A. In Plan A we were out of the bank now, Clara and I in my imagination, and we had gotten the loan! Soon we were building the house together with my father's tools. She was good with the hammer and strong enough to haul the materials. We only brought in outside help to dig the foundation. We did the rest ourselves, with wood from our own land. We'd smile at one another during the hammering and sawing. We were a perfect team. It was beautiful...

Suddenly she brought me back to the Bee Hive, stroking my hair and saying, "I'm pregnant now, Steven Jones."

"I'm not that dumb," I said. "It doesn't happen that fast."

"No, but I know I am."

For a moment I was alarmed. But in a flash I was back in my imagination. And in my mind there came a new aspect to Plan A. She was growing with the house, growing a baby in her belly, and eventually I had to do the heavy work myself, and my father had to lend a hand, while Clara—this made me blush—was in the kitchen heavy with child, chatting with my mother. And they liked each other—not too much, they liked each other just enough. And in Plan A when the baby was born we gave it a name, any name, any name except one. There was only one name we didn't want to call him. Any name but Kevin. Deep into Plan A and unimaginable bliss I wondered what had happened to the little devil, Kevin. Had the story worked? Had he really been exterminated?

"Hi, Dad," Kevin said to me, looking up from his doll.

I rolled over and went to sleep.

ALL RED

The next morning she woke up before me and brought me back some breakfast from McDonald's.

"I got you three Egg McMuffins," she said, smiling.

I ate them in her bed—delicious—as Kevin sucked on a straw from a vanilla milkshake, reluctantly at first, but she had coaxed him on, and eventually he had gotten his mouth wide enough to get around the straw. I didn't think anything of it at first, but as I saw down to the dresser to continue with the story, it came to me. She was weaning him.

All day long I took breaks from writing to think how much I loved her, and to embellish Plan A with embarrassing details: our child's christening at that white Pizza Hut church on the outskirts of town, my parents and Clara's mom and aunt, and yes, her tattooed cousin, looking on reverently as the priest—who looked remarkably like the janitor—splashed water on the baby's head, and we enjoyed it so much that we became churchgoers! Every Sunday she would drive me to that church—on a motorcycle!—with her hair blowing in the wind, and we didn't like the religion as much as we liked the ritual of going, standing silently together in the pew, her hand gently clasping mine. Our religion truly was a private affair, having very little in common with what the priest/janitor spoke about, and yet, everything to do with it. Our religion continued throughout our life. She drew our pictures religiously in the studio I had designed in our house, with big windows offering a view down to the river—that same river I had once practically slept in, afraid of my own house, and she drew magical, impossibly wonderful drawings, and became a famous artist! And I became a famous soybean farmer, and soon we were able to afford that Harley by the sea! We drove there on the weekends sometimes and spent the day tidying up the place, walking by the water, hands clasped, the baby now walking on its own two feet, the three of us a magic family...

But then I became sad. Throughout all the musings now I sensed there was a lurking presence watching the idyllic scenes from above, or below—from somewhere. This lurking presence was snickering, telling me that even these wondrous times didn't matter, and that lurking presence was called Kevin, who could "never be killed." But there must be a way, I thought. There must.

Presently, though, another problem presented itself, and it had to do with the machine and the story I was writing. I had gotten to a point in the story where I had to tell about a man coming to a room just like this one with a bottle of whiskey in order to save a woman just like her from a cup full of poison. Plan A necessitated the revealing of Plan B. I had to tell about it. If I left it out I would be telling a false story. The problem was, Clara kept appearing periodically behind me to look over my shoulder as I typed, reading the story as it approached this incident—the replacing of poison with whiskey—and I wondered if it wasn't time to implement my insurance policy, Plan C.

"You're getting near the end," she said too happily. "We might be able to leave tonight, don't you think?"

"Yes," I said. "But I can't write with you watching over

my shoulder."

She went back to the bed. I typed the part of the story about the poison. But now another problem presented itself. As the sun went down and the evening came, I was running out of things to tell in my story. No matter how fast I typed, it seemed the narrative was catching up with me. I was now writing about a man who comes to a house like the Bee Hive every day to write a story. And then I was writing about a man who makes love with the woman of his dreams. And soon I was writing about this man's problem, how the woman is looking over his shoulder and he can't write about his Plan, which he calls Plan B, which is the plan of replacing poison with whiskey. And that written, I had hardly anything else to tell.

"I'll go to McDonald's for dinner," she said. "Got any more money?"

I handed her a bill.

Kevin didn't go with her. He stayed there on the cot playing with his doll as I typed the little more I was able to type, and when the story caught all the way up to itself I stopped typing and employed at last my insurance, Plan C. I reached my hand into the machine and began spinning the little spool that wound the red and black ribbon across the keys.

"How's it going, Dad?" asked Kevin.

"Fine," I said, turning to eye him on the bed there, looking up at me suspiciously.

"Why are you stopping?"

"I'm not stopping," I said. "The key got jammed."

I turned around and started typing again. Then I stopped, making a frustrated sigh, and stuck my hand back into the machine and spun the ribbon some more. I heard him again, the little boy who up until this time had shown no interest in my typing, speaking with a diabolical, insinuating little voice.

"What's happening, Dad?"

"Nothing, Kev," I said, typing again. I only dared one more time to break off from typing, and this time I got the ribbon spun so that it was almost all the way wound off the spool on the right, while the spool on the left was over-flowing. As I put my fingers back to the keyboard, I knew the ribbon could run out at any time now. I typed slowly. It had to happen with her in the room. She was taking a long time. Kevin was still staring at me from the cot, ignoring his doll now. I typed the story of a man sticking his fingers into the typewriter to make the typewriter ribbon run out. As I typed I prayed to the janitor who was standing in my consciousness with his broom. Please, I begged him.

Please...

At last she returned from McDonald's.

She brought Chicken McNuggets this time, a bucket of forty-eight. They didn't taste like the chicken we raised ourselves on the farm and slaughtered for special meals. They tasted like plastic—wonderful, plastic chicken meat. But after I'd eaten about twenty I felt bloated and depressed and went back to the typewriter.

"Are you almost done?" she asked me after I'd been typing a while longer.

"Yes, let me finish," I said irritably.

"I just wanted to show you my new space suit," she said.

She was standing behind me in a costume that made me shiver. It was all red—red bra and red panties and even red stockings. And behind her Kevin had changed into a new suit, too, made out of red shiny paper, just like the last one, with a cape and a little sword, but all of it red like the horrible shining in his little eyes.

"Don't you like it?" she said.

"It's all red..."

"Don't you understand?"

"No."

"You'll get it," she said. "Eventually..."

She kissed me on the lips, but I felt cold kissing her this time. It wasn't anything like kissing her last night. I turned around and went back to typing. And now I was typing about a woman coming back with Chicken McNuggets, so current was the narrative, like the tortoise catching up to the hare of my typing, and then I was typing about the woman's new underwear, all red, and if Clara read any of it I would be lost. I suppressed the desire to go to the bathroom that the McNuggets had induced in my belly. If I left the room she would read what I'd just typed and all would be lost, but all was lost anyway because there wasn't any more story. I had typed my way to the present.

I had started the story when the man was eight, and now the man was twenty, and the only thing left to describe was him sitting at the typewriter in a state of confusion because his story had ended but still his fingers punched the keys, while a girl lay on the bed, the most beautiful woman in the world, smoking a cigarette and waiting, and everything seemed hopeful in her. Her eyes were lit up with hoping and believing, but the man was in despair because he wanted desperately for the ribbon to run out. But it wouldn't and he had to sit there stalling. How long would it go on? Eventually she would read the last page he had written and he would be discovered for what he was, an artist of deception.

At last my prayers were answered.

POTIONS

Ipunched the keys. Nothing appeared on the page. The keys had jammed. I punched again. Nothing. I fiddled with some dials. Nothing. I fiddled with the spool. Remarkable. It was built so that you could spool it forward, from right to left, but you couldn't spool it back. There was no returning. The ribbon had expired.

"What's the matter?" she asked me.

"The ribbon is all used up."

"No."

"Yes. See for yourself."

She got up off the bed.

"How close are you to the end?"

"Pretty close."

"Let me read it."

"No, it wasn't so good near the end of the ribbon. I'm gonna have to do that part over when we get another ribbon."

"Why?"

"It wasn't working out."

"Let me see!"

"No!" I said, ripping the last page out of the typewriter and turning it over on the stack. "It was no good."

"I'm sure it's fine," she said. "Let me read it."

248

"No."

"You finished the story, didn't you?" she cried. "Didn't you?"

"No."

"Liar! The machine will work now! I know it!"

"No!" I lied.

"Get away from there," she said, pushing me off my seat into a heap on the floor and replacing me at the machine. She put in a clean sheet of paper. She typed something on the typewriter, and I was glad because now she could see for herself that the ribbon had run out. Plan C was working brilliantly. Except for one thing. After she typed what she typed the machine began to glow.

"Yay!" exclaimed Kevin, scrambling off the bed and up the dresser, where he started dancing around.

"Oh my God!" cried Clara, her eyes wide at the sight of the machine glowing there, unreally, in her room, on her real dresser, in front of her real mirror, in the middle of real life. Suddenly the machine seemed to dart back and forth, changing its position on the table.

"How could you lie to me?" she said, her voice far away. "After last night? I thought you wouldn't lie any more after last night!"

"I'm sorry! I didn't know!"

"I don't trust you any more!" she cried. "But then I never did. So it doesn't make any difference."

I stood and looked at the blank paper in the machine. Here in letters that were half black and half red was the word ON, darting back and forth, sticking out from the page, in three dimensions. I thought of typing OFF. That didn't qualify as an effective plan. I thought of coming clean with her, making her read the rest of the story, revealing my other plan, the proposal of marriage, the dream of happiness here together in the real world, but she would hardly be interested in that now, staring as she was in dis-belief at the impossible machine.

"And now," she announced, "the potion!"

She went to her closet.

"What are you doing?" I said, my mind wavering franti-cally along with the machine on the table, not sure of any-thing.

"Getting the potion!"

I looked over at the Slurpee cup as she leafed through her closet.

"That's my potion," she said. "I'm getting yours."

"Mine?"

"I mean, I thought you needed one too, but I wasn't sure. Then the other night when I got so mad at you—do you remember?—that's when I found out for sure. So that's why I had Ernie take me into Grandville, to get a potion for you, because I knew then that you needed one too. This one's yours."

"Mine?" I said again, dumbly.

She had removed a shoebox from the closet from which she took out another Slurpee cup and three white things that looked like normal, white postal envelopes, but in my shaking I couldn't tell. She placed the white things on the cot. Then she picked up "her" Slurpee cup from the night table. She came over to me. She handed me "mine."

"What is it?" I asked, taking the plastic cup.

"It's the potion," she said, as she unbuttoned my shirt with her free hand.

"What are you doing?"

"Showing you," she said. "Just in case you didn't know."

She pulled my shirt out from the front of my trousers.

"I didn't know myself until the other night," she went on. "Until I felt your stomach. And that's why I got so mad. Because I had believed you were different, really I had. But then I realized something. You've been living here such a long time it was bound to happen. It could have happened to you any time. I didn't even need to ask you about it. Or Kevin. I understood. I just needed to get you a potion too. That's all."

She had opened my shirt now and she was pushing her finger into a hole in my belly, and when she took the finger away, I saw it there, sticking its little head out from my fat middle, a little worm of a belly button.

"Ah ha ha," I thought I heard someone laugh. I looked over at Kevin. He wasn't laughing. But I heard him laughing. I remembered my story about the belly button. Of course it had been make believe. I always knew I had a belly button.

"It was just a story," I said to Clara, laughing, but sounding so false all of a sudden. "You know..."

I looked at Kevin again. He was up on the machine now, riding it as if it were a little bucking bronco. Then my eyes shifted to the window. Outside it seemed like sparkles were falling through the blackness of the night. For a minute I believed it... For a minute I thought the whole night was lighting up with a magical power and something I never really believed in was happening, the whole universe was becoming my enchanted dream—a magic boy and an incredible space ship and the most beautiful girl, and a trip to heaven. But then my eyes saw the sparkles outside that window for what they really were. Little crystals falling from the sky. It was snowing.

"It's too early," I thought. "Much too early for snow..."

The soybeans! They would be ruined by the snow. I had meant to take them in that morning with my father. But I hadn't even gone home. My parents must have wondered. They must have walked around all day with shadowy faces, wondering whether they should call. But then, there's no phone in the Bee Hive, so they couldn't call. And they wouldn't have wanted to interfere. Perhaps my father and Lee Roy brought in the soybeans. But no, they wouldn't have done that without me, the proud father of the field. But now it was too late. And too early. The snow was falling. I had to do something to stop it. But there wasn't anything to do. I couldn't stop it snowing. I couldn't save the soybeans. I couldn't cover them with a huge plastic cloth, that wouldn't do any good. It wasn't the snow falling from above that would kill them, it was the frost that would come after, from below, which would harden the roots and crystallize the molecules and then the soybeans would die in the field and there was nothing I could do.

"Let's drink together," she said.

"How do you know it's the right potion?" I whined. "I'm afraid."

"Don't you trust me?"

"Yes... but how can you be sure you didn't make a mistake?"

"Steven Jones," she said. "How could that guy in the story tell?"

"What story?"

"The story about when God came to this guy and told him to burn his only child. How could he know it was really God and not some imposter trying to trick him?"

She must have been reading over my shoulder when I wrote about a man remembering that story. I tried to remember when I wrote that. Maybe it was that afternoon. Or maybe she just knew the story because I knew it. Maybe she knew everything I knew. And I thought about the whiskey in her Slurpee cup. I wondered if it was still whiskey. If she knew about that story she knew about it all...

"But in the end," I said, "God let that guy off the hook. He didn't have to kill his son."

"This will let us off the hook," she said. "This will dissolve the worm. And there won't be any more hooks, and there won't be any more anything."

"But how do you know?"

"Because I know," she shouted, as the light from the machine intensified and Kevin started yelping louder and louder, like a little doll gone berserk with joy.

"And you shouldn't ask me that question. I never doubted you, Steven Jones, even when you deceived me. And I don't think I deserve that kind of question, because this is the one part of the story that I figured out myself. Can't you give me a little credit? Haven't I earned that?"

"Yes," I said.

"Do you trust me?" she shouted, her hair blowing behind her now, as though the machine had brought in a wind from nowhere that was sweeping us both up.

"Yes."

"Do you wanna drink the potion?"

"Yes."

"We don't have to count to three or anything," she shouted. "We'll know when to drink it."

"Yes."

We looked at each other. She was smiling so hopefully that I forgot all my doubts. I stared at her long pale face, and her red hair, which I noticed now had started growing out. There were dark brown hairs at the root of her scalp, pushing out the red. But in her eyes there was joy. I felt I was looking down a microscope and spying on the primary molecule of joy that she was, bubbling over and dancing with life. Then I realized that I was feeling this same joy, and she was looking down the microscope of my eyes into the primary molecule that was me! Suddenly the primary molecules were the same molecule. And the thing inside me was inside her at the same time—defying all laws and being in two places at once. I was her, and I was me. And we were together.

Then at precisely the same moment we began raising the Slurpee cups to our lips, and it was moving too fast now. I didn't have time to think or theorize. I only had time to do what I had to do, put the cup to my lips. For only a flash did I formulate a plan—pretend to drink! Pretend to drink! But right away that became impossible, the thought came too early or too late, I couldn't tell, because I was swallowing the golden water, harsh and sour tasting, burning my throat. In a second I had slugged the whole plastic cupful. And so had she.

We let go of our cups. They fell together toward the floor as though in slow motion in the corner of my vision, which was now plastered onto her vision, and together we were seeing the same thing. Anything that happened now we would experience together. The picture of my parent's broken faces when they learned of my death, standing in a field of frozen soybeans, didn't seem so tragic to me now, because I was with her. I was leaving them behind, and going on to another life, with her, and no matter how awful or brilliant it would be, the important thing was that we wouldn't be alone and we would share it, half and half, two halves of the same thing.

I understood suddenly why she was wearing all red. Because I was wearing all black! And now we formed a perfect line between red and black and we were complete.

I remembered my deception—the whiskey I had poured into the Slurpee she had just guzzled down.

"Clara!" I began, but before I could confess about the trick I had played I thought: how absurd to tell her. She knows everything. Of course she does.

"You did it," she said. "You trusted me. I knew you would."

Her face was turning green, but in my ecstasy I thought it was a voluptuous green, a spectacular green, the green of all time! It wasn't until the sickness seized her and made her convulse that I saw it—the green of poison. She began moaning, doubling over in the wind that was furiously beating the room, falling toward the floor.

"Clara!"

"Mommy!" I heard Kevin cry over the howling wind.

"Clara, what's wrong?"

"The worm," she said, her eyes burning with pain, pain which breathed out at me through her eyes like gas escaping and evaporating in the howling wind. "The worm is dissolving..."

Now the green in her face was turning to a pale blue, and out of her ear there came crawling a trickle of red blood down onto her white neck, as she let out a hideous scream.

"Ooooooooh!"

I was down on the floor above her, my hands clutching her waist, trying to grab her back from the poison possessing her body. Then I remembered. I had drunk a Slurpee too.

"Clara!" I shouted. "It's not working for me! It's not working!"

"No," she yelled, shaking her head, her lips writhing as though it were almost impossible for her to speak now. "No, yours was just vinegar."

"Vinegar?"

"Yes," she said, "I had to go to Grandville for mine. My potion. Because I knew you'd pour it out. I knew you would."

"No!"

"Don't you get it? I'm letting you off the hook!"

"But you're dying!" I shouted.

She laughed, then she moaned again. Then she laughed once more.

"I know that, stupid," she said. "I know."

"No!" I thought to myself. "You didn't have to do this. We could have been happy here. We could have lived with my parents while... And gone to church and held hands at the bank and you would have liked my mom... I love you Clara, not Mara, but you, exactly who you are, I was just afraid to say it... Ashamed... But I loved you so much... And the studio for you to paint in... The baby... It would have been good and you would have believed in it. Not at first. But with the seasons you would have grown into it, and I know you would have believed in it and then one day you'd love me, too... And we'd grow old..."

It was too late for me to say it to her. But I thought it.

"I know," she said then, as though she had heard me thinking.

"Then why?" I thought. "Why do this?"

Kevin was grabbing at his mother's arm, looking upset and... angry, I thought. Kevin had changed. He grew a woman's face, identical to Clara's long pale face, as he grabbed at her. Then he turned back into Kevin, with a little face that looked like my own, and in an instant he flashed back and forth from woman to man a thousand times, as I remembered that lurking presence over all my dreams of happiness with her, the lurking presence that was Kevin, who could never be killed, and would spoil anything we created together. And then I understood why. He was in Clara. And he was in me. And there was no hope.

"I know," she gurgled. "I know."

Then her face went blank. Her body stiffened in my arms.

ME AGAINST KEV

"Mommy!"

Kevin glared at me.

"You killed Mommy!"

I stared back at his vicious eyes. He looked like an angry dog, about to attack me. How absurd, I thought, that I have built my life around this little clot of hate disguised as a gentle little boy. How absurd he seems now. How obscene.

"You killed Mommy!" he growled.

"Shut up!" I shouted, in the same tone Clara had shouted at him when she kicked him across the room. It worked for me, too. He didn't have anything more to say. He just stood there in his absurd paper costume glaring at me harmlessly.

I looked up at the dresser. The machine had stopped glowing. The hurricane of wind had subsided. On the dresser was a regular old typewriter, nothing more. I looked over at the cot, above Clara's body. There were three envelopes on the bed. Picking them up I read the names on each envelope. One said "Mom," one said "Kurt," and the last one had my name on it—"Steven Jones."

I put that one inside my coat as I stared at a pile of papers standing next to the typewriter. They seemed as absurd as Kevin now. They made me feel sick. But for some reason I grabbed them and walked out of the room, and, remembering another story from the past, I didn't look back.

When I got to the front porch I said to her mother: "Something's happened."

Alarm came to her face as she bolted past me into the house, followed by the other lady, who flashed her teeth at me in an accusing grimace as she passed. I walked down the porch steps and got into the car. Kevin made it in just before the door slammed. I drove home through the snowfall, which was letting up now, but had gathered into a couple of inches under the wheels. He didn't say anything for most of the way.

"What are we gonna do now?" he said at last.

"Shut up."

He didn't talk again until I pulled into the driveway. When I stopped to look in the living room window at my parents he whined at me.

"Da-ad," he whined, and his face started filling with pain, his little eyes tearing, as though he knew what I was planning now, in my most secret self.

"Please don't, Dad," he cried.

I looked through the car window at the house. I saw a curtain pulling back. My mother had heard the car pulling up and was peering out through the snowfall.

I got out of the car. Kevin jumped out after me. He didn't back away, but he was sobbing now, pitifully, trying to wheedle sympathy.

I was unmoved. He looked up at me from our driveway, so small compared to my huge body, the most fragile-looking face. He held his hands up to his eyes and begged one last time: "Don't do it, please!"

Now that I couldn't see his face I had no trouble doing it. I had no trouble lifting my boot above his little head and stomping down hard, feeling his little bones crunching on the stones under my heel. I had no trouble listening to his last squeaking "Dad!" dissipating into the lonely night air. And I had no trouble looking at what remained on the stones when I removed my shoe. There upon the white snow was a little splotch of red and yellow tissue inside a tiny shirt and pair of shorts and a red aluminum cape and a little stick which had once been his sword, gnarled inside a tiny piece of skin that must have been his hand. I had no trouble smelling the tiny whiff of death which rose from the ground.

I went to the faucet in the shed and cleaned the tissue off my shoe with a hose. Then I went inside the house.

THE END OF ME AND KEV

Ididn't know what she wrote to her mom or Kurt. But whatever she wrote it was enough for them to leave me out of the rest of the story—her ambulance ride and her death certificate and her trip to the morgue and her burial. I didn't go to the funeral, if there was one. I didn't know.

The next morning my father and I went over the frosted soybeans.

"Whatayou think?" asked my father.

"I think they'll be okay."

That afternoon the sun came up and we brought in the beans. A third of them were hard and had to be disposed of. The rest were saved. I came upstairs to wash after we had finished storing them in the barn. It was while I lay soaking in the bathtub that he reappeared.

"Hi, Dad," he waved from somewhere deep inside me.

He was still dressed in his shorts and his check shirt. I paid no attention to him. I went on with my bath.

"Hi, Dad," he said while I climbed into bed.

I proceeded with my "silent treatment." He seemed to fade deeper into some invisible well as I drifted off to sleep, but I knew he was still there lurking.

When I sat back down at the typewriter a few days later

to finish the story it was for a different purpose. I knew now that no story would ever rid me of Kevin and that lurking presence. I finished the story simply because I had grown addicted to typing over that week at Clara's. My fingers enjoyed twiddling the keys, and it seemed to settle me somehow.

"Hi, Dad," he said as I typed.

I proceeded with the story, ignoring him, until I got to the part about Clara dying. I remembered her face with nobody left in it, like a mask inside fake red hair. I left off typing until the next night when I told the rest of the story.

A few days after her death I received a letter from her cousin, Kurt.

Preacher,

I don't know what happened. But Clara wrote me a note telling me a bunch of stuff. One of the things she asked me to do is to write you this. She asked me to write you and tell you what the doctors found when they did her autopsy. She must have known. The doctors found that inside her the egg and the sperm had conceived, and if she had still been alive she would have been at the very beginning of being pregnant. You and her would have had a child.

Kurt

But even though I can add that part of the story here at the end when I finish this writing, Kevin will still be in there, watching and telling me that this is another waste of time in the Land of Worms and that maybe I should do what Clara did. Or maybe I should go out there into the barn and spit on those soybeans because nothing I could ever create could be worth anything. Or maybe I should hide myself from my mother and father and from the world, and maybe I should sleep more, because when I'm asleep it's at least tolerable. Or maybe I should just keep on trudging around through life, because it'll be over soon anyway. Or maybe...

It goes on and on. He doesn't say anything except "Hi, Dad," now. That's all I let him say. But I hear it all in that little voice. I hear how much he suffers and I hear him telling me what a mistake it is that we're even alive, me and Kev. Me and Kev. It goes on and on...

I don't expect this story to change anything, and I don't expect anything magical to occur when I finish entering this "code," now that the narrative has caught up with the present, except that she will come back to me for a moment, and it will be like being with her again, and we will be connected, Clara and I and the child we were going to have, because the last thing I'm writing is the letter she left me in the envelope marked "Steven Jones."

CLARA'S STORY

Dear Steven Jones

If you're reading this letter then everything worked out according to my story. I am free from her at last. Clara Price is dead. Maybe before she died I found out if you trusted her enough to go on this voyage with me. That's all I wanted to know. You might have seen me then. The angels came and took me back to where I belong. I'm sure you were upset, though, because I left you all alone. I wish you could have come with me but you were meant to stay here. Maybe you were meant to make something out of this life. I don't know. And now you're a long way from me and even though I miss you I accept the fact that some things aren't possible... yet. That's the great thing about this place I'm in now. Even if I miss you I know I'll be seeing you soon. I'll be seeing everyone I loved while I was called Clara Price, because in this place all dreams come true. So don't be lonely. Maybe you'll be lucky and find out what it is you were meant to do there in the Land of Worms. Or maybe you'll even find a potion that really does dissolve the worm! But even if you don't, don't worry, because in this place even the worms are loved. If they weren't perfect worms they never would be allowed to come here and drag people back to wormland in the first place. That's why I don't want you to be too hard on Kevin. Just let him be what he is, and you be what you are. It doesn't matter. It's like a guy you know found out once, that nothing really matters and it's all just a crazy mixed-up dream.

Love

Me

PS Love to Kevin. I'll be seeing you both real soon.